#

Rose and the Secret Passage

Phyllis A. Collmann

ISBN: 978-1-57579-431-0

Library of Congress Control Number: 2010912104

For additional copies of this or other
books written by Phyllis Collmann:
phyllisacollmann@hotmail.com
712-540-4082
www.collmannwarehouse.com

Second printing 2014

Printed in the United States of America

PINE HILL PRESS
4000 West 57th Street
Sioux Falls, SD 57106

Dedication

To my husband, Colin,
for fifty-eight years of marriage and for his
consistency of love, strength, and caring.

To my children
Cynthia, Kimberly, Ronald and Melonie.
I love you dearly.

To all my grandchildren
and great-grandchildren.
I will love you forever.

About the Author

Phyllis A. Collmann is a retired nurse. She lives on a farm in northwest Iowa, with her husband of fifty-eight years. They has also begun living part-time in Chicago. While living on the same farm for forty-five years, she continues to write about the Rose Donlin series. This seventh book in the series is a continuation of Rose's adventure.

The Series of Rose Donlin Helgen:
Rose's Betrayal and Survival
Rose's Triumphant Return
Rose's Heart's Decision
Rose's Dream Fulfilled
Rose's Unexpected Tragedy
Rose's Nightmare Returns
Rose and the Secret Passage

Other books written by Phyllis:
Kim's Unplanned Sega
Mother's Innocence Proven
Christmas At Our House

A Very Special Thank You

To my dear friend Julie Ann Madden.

To Kimberly Ann Bonnett and
Melonie T. Collmann Luban.

To Dr. Jeffrey S. Luban, DPT., COMT.
for helping name this book.

To Jody Sitzmann for the book cover
background scene taken at his Century Farm.

To Ron Collman of Plattsmouth, Nebraska
for taking all the photographs.

To Allen Leekley, Wyatt Brink, and Gerrit Brink.

Chapter 1

Cook was a very complex man. He always preferred to be alone. His thoughts were his own, never expressing any private details of his life to anyone. His young youth years were happy until he turned fifteen, and his life was never the same. He was born in a sod house in the rolling hills of South Dakota. The sod home he lived in with his parents was the only happiness he had ever had.

His parents told him their life story so when the time came he could tell his family. But, he never married to pass on the story. The love he found, he could not marry her. The team and wagon his parents had were given to his father by his grandfather whom he never met. The young couple left their home during the night, as her parents forbid her to ever see his father again. It was too late; they were in love.

While traveling they stopped in a small town and were married by a Justice of the Peace. They continued to travel through the bad lands of South Dakota, not knowing where they were. They stopped on some promising land to farm. On the land they found a hill in which to dig their home.

They had a hoe, pitchfork, and a shovel. His father also had boards, a hammer, and nails to reinforce the dirt ceiling. The dirt dug from the new sod home was thrown into the wagon and hauled away so when it rained they would not have mud outside the door.

The digging took all day and night for nearly three weeks. His father was determined to get his new bride a home of their own. The young couple slept under the wagon until the digging was finished. Then it took a few more days to reinforce the ceiling so it would not collapse while they were asleep.

Cook's father would stop each day long enough to hunt food for supper. His mother learned how to skin a rabbit, start a fire and place the rabbit on a sturdy limb that hung over the fire. The meat was so well done it would fall apart on their plate.

The long tiresome days slowly passed. The work of digging was hard, and the dirt was heavy. The site they picked for their home was made for several reasons. The land would be cleared, then, plowed up with the only tools he had, and planted to corn, oats, and a large garden. Everything was done by hand.

The creek was a short distance to get fresh water every day. They also chose another place to bathe in and wash their clothes. The creek continued to flow. The fresh water was cold and clear. The place they chose to homestead gave the young couple everything they needed to survive. They told their son how happy they were together. They were so much in love.

Chapter 2

This was where Albert (Cook) was born, and when Albert was about four years old, his parents began to tell him stories about their life and the long trip here to start their life together. About digging their home and most of all, the reason they left their parent's home at a very young age.

Albert was fifteen years old when the flu epidemic struck their area in South Dakota. His mother suddenly became ill with a cough and then she developed a high fever. She complained of her body aching, and within a day she had stopped eating. Albert's father never left his mother's side day or night. He tried all of the old remedies he could think of, nothing worked.

It was exactly two weeks, and Albert's mother died on a cold, dreary, rainy night in the fall. It happened while Albert was sleeping. He woke to hear a noise he had never heard before. He quietly crawled out of bed and slipped over to where the noise was coming from. His father was lying next to his mother holding her tenderly in his arms, sobbing. Albert returned to his bed knowing his father would come to tell him when he was ready.

Albert's father dressed his wife in the best dress she had. Then he slipped her wedding band off of her finger and slowly turned, handing it to Albert. They wrapped her in a blanket and laid her in a wooden box his father had made from scraps of lumber. His father chose her grave site on top of a hill near the sod house. Standing next to the grave they could look out over a large valley. The two people she loved more than life dug her grave.

The breeze blew gently on them as each threw the dirt away. The lone tree stood a few feet away. The birds whistled loudly, not knowing the sadness in the hearts of the two men below. Lowering the wooden box was the hardest thing Albert and his father ever had to do. Albert tried not to be emotional in front of his grieving father. This was the beginning of an unwelcome change in the life of Albert and his father.

Nothing would change the valley or the creek. Water would flow as usual, like it had for the fifteen years they had been here. The trees, the birds and animals living in the area, but the life of the two men had changed. Nothing would ever be the same for them. Prayers were said as they covered the grave. Albert had offered to make a cross and place it on his mother's grave.

Chapter 3

Days dragged by slowly. They each tried to keep busy. Albert and his father loaded the wagon with corn to take into the nearest town. His father always started early in the morning and would arrive home just in time for supper.

Nothing would be different except he would not bring a small gift home for his wife from the general store this trip. And his supper would be prepared by Albert. They ate their supper in silence like they did every night. Albert's father remained silent the following days. He had developed a set pattern. He left the sod house after breakfast and did not return until dark. That night Albert waited for him before he finally ate his own meal and then went to bed.

The following morning Albert dressed and started the cook stove to get their oatmeal for breakfast. The coffee perked while the oatmeal cooked. He put tin cups and bowls on the table.

Then he walked into his father's bedroom. Albert opened his mouth to tell him to come to the table—but the bed was empty. He pulled the covers back to the bottom of the bed to make sure his father was not there.

Albert looked over all of their land and could not find him. He knew wherever his father had gone he rode on one of the horses that pulled the wagon.

Chapter 4

Albert decided his father needed time alone to grieve for the love of his life. Albert stayed alone in the sod house the rest of the long cold winter. His food was getting low in the cave when spring finally arrived.

Albert plowed the land with the one horse he had. He planted the corn crop with seed he had shelled by hand from ears of the best corn ears he had kept from last year's crop. The days were long and tiresome for him. He hoped he had done a good job putting the crop in. He wanted his father to be proud of him.

The first thing he did each morning was place his fishing pole in the creek. The food he had on hand was getting low and he had no way of getting more. He had no money to buy any at the general store. The fish were plentiful, so he could survive. He had watched and learned to fish. Also, he had gone hunting with his father.

He found things to do during the day just to keep busy, and he always looked for his father's approval. He wanted to be ready when his father returned. He cut down trees to clear land his father had mentioned farming. Albert would wrap a rope around the fallen tree and then his horse would pull it to where he lined them up to be cut up later for firewood.

He got leaves and debris from a wooded area and packed it around and over the stumps of the trees he had cut down. He had learned from his father to swiftly rub dry sticks together to start a spark. First, the leaves smoldered then in time began to burn.

He checked his fishing pole and removed a nice sized fish, replacing the pole for his supper. The fish was cleaned exactly like his mother had taught him and laid it in the same pan his mother always cooked their fish. He flipped the fish over several times until it was done. Sitting down to eat was when he started to think how good it would be to see his father. If only his mother had not gotten sick. Each night, Albert sat alone in the dark. His thoughts were always the same. Why did his own father leave him this way after just losing his mother?

He only knew two people in his short life. He had never talked to another human being other than his parents. Off in the distance, he could hear a coyote cry for her mate. It was a lonely eerie sound. He fell asleep thinking he could hear his parents whispering to each other before they fell asleep.

The next morning was nearly the same as the morning before and the morning before that. After he ate his fish and washed his pan, he stood for a minute thinking he heard a horse whinny. His first thought was his father had returned. Then he heard another horse whinny before the first horse stopped his whinny.

With no hesitation he ran to his horse, grabbed the wire pulling it over the post. His horse was only a few steps away eating an ear of corn from an old box his father had made from scraps of wood left from reinforcing the sod house. At the same time one hand was slipping around the halter and one hand picked up an ear of corn to coax his horse to come with him. He ran pulling his horse to the sod house. He could hear voices getting closer.

The sod house door was always left open during the day for fresh air. He pulled his horse directly into the opening reaching out and shutting the door, then latched it. He put his horse in the farthest corner from the door and gave him an ear of corn to eat. His hope was the men would think the place was abandoned.

His father's gun was hanging over the door just where his father had left it. He had shot his father's gun while hunting an animal, but never a man.

He shut the door as quietly as he could and put the brace over the handle. He could hear voices getting louder. The words he heard were the words his mother had told him never to say. His father said them while they were working together, if something went wrong like the time a tree fell in the wrong direction and just missed Albert. But he was not allowed to say them.

"Hey, you inside, open the door or I'll shoot it full of holes." The voice was loud and rough sounding.

The gun in Albert's hand was loaded. He stood up against the dirt wall behind the door. They were close enough for Albert to hear the horses breathing heavily and he could smell the horses sweat. He left the wall and took a few steps to reach out in the dark and wrap his hand tightly on his horse's halter.

The gun shot from the intruders was loud coming through the closed door. It left a big gaping hole, big enough for a small animal to crawl through. The bullet whizzed by Albert and lodged in the dirt wall making dirt pieces in chunks fall to the floor.

Albert was nearly pulled off of his feet when his horse jerked his head up high. Albert had grown so fast in the last six months he was tall, lean but very strong. He held on and pulled the horse's head back down.

Then Albert heard one of the men's voices saying, "Let's go, there's no one here."

Albert stood silent, holding on to his horse listening as the two riders rode away. He opened the door slowly and looked out in the direction he thought the riders went. He would never forget the voice of each man. Albert pulled his horse out of the sod house and put her back in the corral. He fed and watered her. He found boards to repair the holes in the door. It was at this time he decided he could not stay and live here alone. Everything in his life had changed.

Chapter 5

The corn field he had carefully taken care of, weeding, and repairing the wagon to haul the corn in. This year he would have to harness the one horse up to the wagon and pick the corn and throw the ears of corn into the wagon. His father had always taken care of everything before.

The days slipped by, and he knew he needed to start early in the morning to be able to fill the wagon. He took no breaks, working every minute of the day and late into the evening until it became dark. In the morning, he walked the horse pulling the wagon toward the trail for an early start. The one horse would have a big load to pull by herself.

Albert unloaded the wagon after the buyer in the nearby settlement told him what he would pay him for a full load. After Albert arrived back home, he parked the wagon next to the row he would pick first in the morning as it was dark.

Eating his fish filled him up. He had lost weight after his mother died. Albert crawled into bed with his clothes on while his feet hung over the end of his bed. His father had made his bed when he was a small boy. He wanted to sleep in his father's bed; it was much longer and his feet would not hang over. Albert had grown so fast, he was over six feet tall at fifteen years old. But what if his father came home? He wanted everything perfect for his father's homecoming. His sleep was restless and filled with small disturbing dreams.

He woke in the morning hearing a horse, then he heard voices, the voices sounded like the two men who had been there before and had shot a hole in the sod house door. Then he heard his horse whinny.

Albert jumped out of bed and opened the door only far enough to see his horse being led away by two men. He could see each had a rifle on their saddle. He started out of the door carrying his rifle as his horse was being pulled out onto the trail by the two thieves.

They had not seen his horse the first time they were here. By the time they reached the trail they were galloping. Albert stood for a minute undecided what to do. If he ran after his horse, he was sure they would shoot him. The two men would never reason with him.

Albert looked at the corn field not knowing what to do. If only his father was here. He'd know what to do. Even empty, pulling the wagon was very difficult. First, he pulled it to the end of the corn row. He sat down on the ground to think it over. He then pulled the wagon next to the sod house door. Hiding the door from any more intruders with the wagon in front of the door no one could tell the sod house was there.

Picking the ears of corn with a pail then carrying the full pail to the wagon, Albert knew it would take at least three more days before he finished the corn field. The last day it started to rain about mid-morning. He continued to pick until he was finished. Covering the corn in the wagon took him longer to find leaves and brush, and when he finally went into the sod house his clothes were wet to his skin, and he was shaking from being so cold.

After removing all of his clothing and redressing, he crawled into bed and covered up with the patch work quilt his mother had made just for him. Without being aware, the tears ran down his face. He began to sob. He stopped long enough to remember hearing the same sound the night his mother died; his father awakened him with the same sound. Albert had not cried in front of his father because his father was so grief stricken. So, he would cry only when he was alone.

Albert woke in the morning feeling sad and so lonely. He opened his mother's night stand, which was a wooden box his father had brought home filled with apples. He reached for his mother's Bible. He put it in his shirt pocket over his heart.

Albert walked to the door, opened it and did not look back after closing the bullet-holed door. He walked up the hill to his mother's gravesite, lowered his body to his knees. He solemnly promised his mother he would return someday. He also promised his mother he would find his father. After picking up his bedroll, he started on his life's journey.

Chapter 6

Albert drifted all of his life until he rode onto Rose Donlin Helgens' homestead. He had worked and saved his money. He did not go into town to drink after getting paid like the rest of the cowhands. He stayed and worked for awhile, then moved on through South Dakota.

He never tired of working in the field or branding calves. But because of his youth and being a loner, he was picked on. He again stayed a couple months and then moved on. The first homestead in Nebraska needed a cook. Albert offered to cook. He had heard some arguing and cussing when he rode into camp. He felt sure he would be beaten up or some crazy cowboy after a night of drinking would end up shooting him. He had watched his mother make biscuits and gravy while the bacon fried. He did everything he could to please the cowhands, starting at 4:00 a.m. The cowhands were rough and tough but they ate till the food was gone. They acted better towards him when they were full.

He stayed only a month, and then moved on again after getting paid. He still did not have enough to buy a horse and saddle yet. Albert walked on to the next homestead. By the end of the day his feet were hurting from his father's old boots as he had out grown his own boots. He sat down along the edge of the dirt road. He rubbed his sore feet and realized he had blisters. He turned his socks upside down and slipped them on hoping to protect anymore blisters from forming and hoping the ones he had would not break and make open sores. It took a day of walking. He could see lights off in the distance and decided to sleep among some trees, then entered the camp in the morning. He was glad to see the sun come up as the night noises kept him awake most of the night. He walked in carrying his only possessions. His youthful look was fading. Cook was looking like a mature man. His face whiskers had started to become thicker and dark as his hair. His hair had not been cut for a few years, it was long and he tied a piece of leather around it and pulled it back and it hung down his back.

He asked for a cook or a cook's helper. He did not get either and was disappointed. The boss said, "The only work I have is to clean the barn with a pitch-fork." Albert spent the next two days cleaning the barn stalls. No one paid any attention to him and no one talked to him. He was lonely and felt like crying. He stayed long enough to get a pay check, then left. He kept his money strapped inside by his stomach. He was so tired of walking and thought he had just enough money to buy a horse. Earning money for a saddle would take longer. He had learned to ride a horse bareback so he thought he could ride bareback from one homestead to the next. It was a long trip across Nebraska and he kept on going into Kansas. The work did not bother him. He did whatever he was asked to do. It was the most lonely he had ever felt. The only one he talked to was the horse he was finally able to buy. Later after working at a lot of homesteads, he was able to buy a saddle

Chapter 7

Five years had passed when he entered the Oklahoma territory. He was only twenty years old but felt as if he'd lived a whole life time. He'd gone from a young boy to an independent man. Albert had no idea where he was or who he was about to meet when he rode onto Rose Donlin Helgens' homestead.

He rode his horse up to Rose's porch as she stepped out of her cabin door. To Albert, she was the most beautiful woman he had ever seen. He didn't look around like he usually did. Albert starred at Rose.

"I'm looking for a job." Albert said nervously.

"Can you cook? I need a cook now." Rose was adamant about finding a cook at this time. Rose and Inga had been doing extra cooking to help the cook out in the bunkhouse. He had been complaining of feeling sick for over a week.

"Yes, yes, I can cook." Albert said in a loud firm voice.

"You can begin," as she pointed to the bunkhouse kitchen.

"What do people call you?" Rose asked with relief in her voice.

"Cook, I go by Cook." Albert answered. He moved his horse toward the bunkhouse not wanting to tell her any more about himself. He rode slowly to the big bunkhouse where the kitchen was located on one end. The kitchen had a large black cast iron stove. The kitchen was orderly, and everything was in place just like Cook liked.

Chapter 8

Cook liked a few people he cooked for and Frank was one. Frank always took time to talk to him or ask if he could do something for him.

Frank's decision not to tell Cook about the squatter family turned out to be a bad decision. The first meeting was torture for Cook.

Frank took care of all the details for the squatter family, then went into Cook's kitchen and asked Cook to go into Oklahoma City's general store and fill the wagon with food supplies. Cook had no idea why so much food was ordered or needed. But Frank was good to him and Cook wanted to do his job right.

When Cook arrived back at the Helgens' homestead, he directed the team to the food storage room connected to the kitchen. He could easily carry the supplies in and put them on the shelves he wanted them on, in order, so he could find the food he planned for each meal. Frank was standing in the doorway. He had a funny smile on his face.

"I forgot to tell you something." Said Frank trying hard to convince Cook the ten children would be no trouble at all.

The door suddenly filled up with ten kids pushing and shoving Frank out of the way, then they all turned and jumped up on the wagon and climbed over the boxes of food, screaming and hollering. The little girls were giggling and clapping their hands together in happiness. Frank hollered, "This is what I wanted to tell you." Still smiling hoping it would help.

Nothing would quiet the kids down. They had never seen so much food. Cook sat in disbelief of what he was seeing. The older boys handed the boxes down to the littler kids and they carried them in and put the boxes on any shelf they could reach. The boxes were not in order. Each of the box labels could not be seen immediately. He would have to turn each box and then stacks of boxes were mixed up. Cooks reaction was exactly like Frank envisioned it to be.

Cook had never seen so many unruly children. Cook sat on his buckboard seat with his mouth partially open, wanting to yell, but nothing came out. He was only able to sit and watch ten children react to happiness, loudness and being out of control.

Not one box of food was in order. The wagon was nearly empty and Cook was still sitting. Frank was still yelling. "The kids belong to Harry and Berta. They were squatters, Rose asked them to come here."

Cook slowly climbed down from the wagon and standing in front of him was the youngest girl with her big brown eyes and long dark hair.

She said, "Hi, my name is Betsy, what's yours?"

Cook didn't answer at first, and then said, softly, almost not wanting to answer. "Cook, People call me Cook."

Frank watched Cook go from hard and angry to soft by a tiny little girl.

Chapter 9

The cowhands rode slumped over with their heads down. They were returning from their long hard search for Wilber Kolveck. Wilber Kolveck had caused so much pain and heartache for Henry and Rose. He was the man that first rescued Henry from drowning in the raging creek flash flood. And then Wilber Kolveck took Henry to his big white house and kept him prisoner for seven months.

They were all tired, dirty, and very hungry. Each one rode up to the new bunkhouse, thinking of a good hot meal and then crawling into a warm bed.

Frank met them at the door and explained loudly to each one. "There's been a change. We found a family in the north forty living in the old squatter cabin. We need the bunkhouse a few nights for them."

"Where are you putting us, Frank?" asked one cowboy sounding angry and full of frustration.

"Why do they need the whole bunkhouse?" one other cowboy yelled. The cowboys all wanted to say how they were feeling. They sat on their horses looking at Frank like they could hit him while feeling like this. Frank finally told them about Harry and Berta with their ten children. The men then sat silent but Frank could hear several men saying, "Ten Kids."

One cowhand sitting on his horse in the back yelled, "Where are we going to sleep?"

Frank answered slowly saying, "In the barn, just for a few nights until we can find a cabin for this large family."

"In the barn, you can't expect these men to sleep in the cold barn." The foreman yelled. "Do we eat in the barn too?" another cowhand yelled.

"No, of course not," Frank said, "As soon as Cook gets the supplies sorted, he'll make supper for everyone."

Another cowhand shouted loudly, "You mean it's not ready, Frank?" All the cowhands looked at each other and then solemnly turned and in single file headed to the barn. As they rode off Frank could hear them all mumbling, "Damn Kids."

What Frank was not aware of was, behind him standing in the bunkhouse with their backs up against the wall were four of the oldest boys of Harry and Berta. They listened to every word. Someone was going to pay.

Chapter 10

Each child had their own bunk. The four boys picked the bunks closest to the back door where Frank had stood. The only sound in the bunkhouse after dark was heavy breathing. But not everyone was asleep.

Walter, the oldest brother, tiptoed and quietly woke his other brothers, Gerrit, Wyatt, and Brandon. Without a word, they slipped out of their bunks. Each carried his boots to the door. Walter opened the door only wide enough for each to pass through. Then he carefully closed the door. Walter led the boys around the barn to the corral where all the horses stood resting. Each boy climbed over the fence into the pen. Walter hugged the fence walking to the big gate that led out into the large pasture where the large cattle herd was. He climbed over the gate easily, unlatched it and pulled it completely open.

Everything was going as planned. Walter whistled and the three boys walked as close as they could to the corral fence, so not to get stomped on or spook the horses. They started to click their tongues to start the horses moving. The horses in the back pushed the horses in the front of them and then all of the horses moved to the gate. Once the first couple of horses were free they began to run, the rest followed and within minutes the corral was empty.

The boys snickered as they went back toward the bunkhouse. Each removed their boots. Walter opened the door for each of his brothers to slip in. Each crawled into their bunk and quickly fell asleep.

Chapter 11

Katy saw a difference in her parents. They enjoyed helping Cook. Now their family was getting enough to eat and never had to share the food on their plate. Now there was always enough food. Rose Donlin Helgens was the answer to her family's prayer. Rose had opened her homestead to a family she had never met before.

Katy was a strong, smart girl, full of love for her family. She was looked up to by all of her family. Katy was older in wisdom than she was in years. Only one other person knew about the four young sons of Harry and Berta. That was Katy, and she would never tell. She lay awake waiting for her brothers to come back into the bunkhouse. Katy knew how the boys felt being moved from their home even if it was a shack. They had been free, and they loved their freedom. Katy was happy because she wanted more in her life. Since coming here she saw the wonderful bunkhouse, clean sheets. She could bathe by herself as her body was changing.

Katy vowed to keep their pranks a secret unless they hurt someone. It would be then she would tell on them. She always thought of herself as a caretaker. But she was also a leader.

Chapter 12

Morning came so fast for everyone because Cook was up early and he expected every cowhand to be up and ready to eat breakfast at 4:00 in the morning. The cowhands were half-dressed coming into the kitchen and each one was crabby. They hadn't slept well on the barn floor.

Then, half way through the cowhands' breakfast, someone came running into Cook's kitchen and yelled, "Our horses are gone, not one left in the corral. The gate is open. They headed up into the rugged area of rocks and trees."

"How did they get out of the corral?" one excited cowboy yelled almost screaming. "How did they get the gate open?"

Each man turned and looked at the man standing next to him with a questioning look on his face. Each wondering if they were guilty of doing this horrible act, not just to one cowhand but to all of them.

No one was aware that the door into the bunkhouse was open a small amount. The only ones interested in listening to the voices coming from Cook's kitchen were four young boys. The boys made no noise; they simply had a smile on their face. The boys went back to their clean bunks and pulled the warm covers over on themselves and immediately fell asleep.

Henry woke to hearing loud knocking on his back door of his cabin. After opening the door he looked into the eyes and faces of his very upset and distressed cowhands. He stood listening about all of their horses missing.

Henry instructed one good rider, Frank, to saddle up Rose's magnificent horse and bring back all of the missing horses.

Henry's voice changed. It sounded almost angry. He was not the type of man to show a temper but a horse was a man's treasure.

He then asked the question, "Who opened the gate? It would take more than one man to do it. And how was it no one heard the horses leave?"

Every cowhand wanted and did answer, yelling and answering at the same time. All Henry heard were words in anger.

"It wasn't any of us. Maybe it was those damn kids" Someone in the crowd yelled. This was the first time Henry heard anyone speak about the squatter's family. Frank listened to the men but didn't say anything. He hadn't told anyone about his meeting with the kids, and what he knew they were capable of doing. And the length they would go to do it. Frank, Jay, and Thomas rode out to round up the cowhands' horses.

Chapter 13

All ten children had wondered over Rose Donlin Helgens' homestead. They were free to go wherever they wanted. Each day they went farther than the day before. After they excitedly saw the old red rooster, they were all curious about him. They followed the rooster around until the rooster turned and chased the kids flying up at them, showing them its long sharp spurs. It was after the noon meal, and the kids all knew their mother and father were helping Cook clean up the kitchen, washing and drying the many dishes.

The older children went back to find the big old red rooster. When they got close, the rooster turned opening up one of his wings then defiantly starting after them. They all yelled and split up and ran in different directions. The rooster continued running in one direction and then another, mostly after the older boys. The older boys were fast and teased him, until the old rooster stopped and turned away.

It was then one of the four older boys had a great idea. He explained they had to find a way to catch the old rooster. This was not going to be easy but now they had a plan. They all

chased and herded him into Joseph's corral and then into the barn. Getting scratched was not going to stop them. It took all the boys to grab him and hold him.

The gunny sack went over his head. At the same time one of the older boys held his scaly old legs with spurs that felt like knifes. One boy tied the rope tightly around and around the legs. The rooster was drug in the bag to Rose's barn while the cowboys were all out working. The rest of the children were told to watch so no one saw what they were doing. Once in the barn, they put him in a manger and left the sack over his head and his feet tied. They would return after dark.

That night all the cowhands were asleep on their bedrolls in the barn. The snoring was about as loud as it could get. No one heard the barn door open slightly and just two boys slipped in. It was very dark but each boy knew exactly where they were going and each knew what they were to do. Together, they lifted the old red rooster out of the manger. At the same time one untied his legs and another lifted off the gunny sack. Not knowing where he was going, the old red rooster ran toward the sleeping, snoring cowhands.

The rooster ran over several sleeping cowboys, digging into their bodies as he went from one to another. They woke yelling and swinging their arms. In the darkness it was chaotic. Stumbling, pushing, falling and getting spurred until one cowhand opened the door and a small amount of light came in. The old red rooster ran out into the night, hurrying off towards Joseph's homestead. The cowhands were all mad and now unable to get back to sleep. They were doing what they had done before. Each was blaming the other. The words coming out of their mouths were the words Cook's mother had taught him not to say.

Chapter 14

Rose thought today would be a good day to go to the bunkhouse and meet Harry, Berta, and their ten children. She took care of her own children first, giving Inga instructions on their naps. Rose knocked lightly on the bunkhouse door while hearing the strangest noise. The noise was a squeaking then a high pitched squealing sound followed.

The high pitched squeal of giggling, and then she heard boys yelling loudly. Rose knocked again and no one opened the door. She reached for the door latch and turned it slowly. Pushing only slightly, she opened it just far enough to see in.

The sight was unexpected. On ten bunks, each bunk held one child, and each child was jumping straight up as high as they could jump. Even the small tiny girl was leaping in the air, so very unafraid.

When they saw Rose each one stopped jumping and stepped down and stood by their bed. Just then the kitchen door opened. Harry and Berta walked in from the kitchen. They each knew who this lovely lady was, and each was so happy to see Rose. Berta put her arms completely around Rose, even knowing Rose was close to giving birth. She was so grateful for what Rose had done for her family.

Harry introduced each of his children to Rose and told her one thing about each child making each one special.

Rose smiled and tried to remember their names. The children all gathered around Rose and each wanted to hug her. Mostly the girls wanted to touch her stomach. Nine-year- old Katy asked when her baby was due to be born. Then, asked if she could help in the birth. Eight- year-old Gilda asked if she could rock the baby after it was born. Seven-year-old Stella asked if she could give the baby its bottle.

Suddenly Rose realized these young girls had helped in the birth and care of the younger siblings. They had been included in the birth to bring them all closer together, unlike Dora Kolveck. Dora did not know her mother was having a baby until her brother, Wilber was born.

Rose thought for a minute, then, said, "I have a wonderful Indian midwife that delivers all of my babies.

Stella yelled, "Father and Katy delivered all of us. We can help father with yours."

Rose quickly put her arms out gently pushed her way through the children, and toward the door saying, "Thank you, I'll let you know." Outside Rose took a deep breath and said out loud, "This family is so strong and determined."

As she walked back to her cabin Rose thought, the children had never been to school. Their mother had home schooled them but did it without books. Rose's mind wondered for a minute and thought about Dora. She had heard so many people in the settlement of Kolveck tell her how brilliant Dora had been in school.

Chapter 15

Wilber Kolveck woke up in the "room" early while it was still dark out, wanting to go upstairs and into the kitchen for fresh water. He had not shaven or had his hair cut for a long time because Dora had always cut it. He had not changed his clothes since coming home. He also needed a bath. Dora Kolveck always slept with her bedroom door closed and Wilber knew it. So, slipping quietly up the stairs into the kitchen for a jar of water was easy. The bread was always stored in the bread box and Wilber knew this too. He took the rest of the loaf of bread along with a few cookies off of a plate setting on the table that Dora had planned on taking to Aunt Olive.

He then headed down the hall to his bedroom. It looked the same so he knew where everything was. He gathered up clean clothes, his night shirt, razor, and found a pair of scissors. Wilber also took another quilt off his bed, as the "room" in the basement was always cold at night. Wilber headed for the pantry, opening it up wide forgetting about how badly the door squeaked. The pantry was located just below Dora's bedroom.

Dora woke suddenly hearing a squeaky noise, and it sounded just like the pantry below her. Dora crawled out of bed while wrapping a blanket around her. She lit her lamp and started down the steps. Below her Wilber heard her coming down the steps.

He remembered the game they used to play, and he thought this was what Dora was playing. He stepped back behind the pantry door and had a big smile on his face. Dora looked around and saw no one. She decided morning was near, so returned to her room to dress for the day to search for Wilber.

After Wilber returned to the "room" he felt good. He thought he had won the game and quickly ate his four cookies he had taken. Wilber laughed out loud.

Chapter 16

Wilber had opened the cave door attached to the big white house and did not need a light he knew each step down under the house. He started toward the "room" that had been his punishment room. He decided to stay in it the first night, and then he would check out the tunnel to hide in.

He and Dora had discovered the tunnel one day after their parents had both died. They were playing the game Wilber always wanted to play. Dora always did whatever Wilber asked her to do. She always wanted him to be happy. The tunnel was a small crawl space behind a trunk stored in the fruit room under the big white house. Dora had always refused to enter it, leaving Wilber begging and pleading with her. She very seldom refused him but that time she firmly refused. Dora was so afraid she would get stuck, as it looked so small in size.

Dora knew where the tunnel started but did not know where it ended; only Wilber knew that. The first time he crawled through, it was dirty and full of spider webs. It did not bother Wilber at all. He finally had a secret no one else but Dora knew about it, and it was all his.

Dora had learned in school why some people had tunnels built under their homes. She remembered her father's explanation when she asked him. At the time she did not know about the one under her home.

"People who were outcasts or people who were hiding knowing they would be shot if caught during the war, hid in the tunnel," her father told her. He did not tell her he had a tunnel, but told her some people helped by opening their homes to hide them. Now Wilber Kolveck was using the tunnel.

Dora thought back and never remembered anyone coming into their home. She thought about studying in school about what was called the Civil War in 1850. Now Wilber Kolveck was using the tunnel. Dora left the big white house and went directly to the barn. The team stood quietly while she harnessed them. Unaware, only a few feet away Wilber was watching.

Wilber got to the hay manger and then climbed over it and headed to the door. He couldn't have been happier. The game was more fun than he had ever imagined. With Dora leaving and out of the house, he knew he could take whatever he needed and hide in the tunnel.

The following morning Dora sat at the table eating her usual breakfast of dry oatmeal and thinking if only she could find him. She couldn't help but think something was not right. She was sure the water pail was full when she went to bed. She also remembered having a full loaf of bread out to cut and she knew she had bread left from breakfast the morning before. It also seemed to her that there were fewer cookies on the plate she had planned on giving Aunt Olive. Dora realized how very tired and worried she was over Wilber's disappearance.

Maybe she just imagined it all. But she did not imagine. That night Wilber crawled through the tunnel as soon as it was dark. He got to the hay manger, climbed over it and headed to the door. The game had never been this much fun. The Kolveck town was only one-half mile away and all the lamps or lanterns were out. He walked as fast as he could and felt good. Wilber tried to open the back door of the general store from behind in the alley. The door he could get open was a shed standing behind the general store.

Wilber took a shovel, a pail and a lantern. This was all he could carry the half-mile back to the tunnel. When he was ready, he thought he could make the tunnel larger. He stored his stolen items in the tack room and covered them with some old worn-out horse blankets.

By the time he returned home, he needed to go to sleep. Tonight he slept in the tunnel for the first time on the quilt from his bed.

Chapter 17

The following day started in Rose's cabin as usual except for one thing. Rose was sure her baby would be born soon. Henry had gotten up before Rose was awake. He could hear

Inga trying to dress the children. Her German accent was coming in clear. And then she would speak to them in German. Rose had mentioned to Henry she preferred the children learn English first. Henry tapped lightly on the door and stepped into the children's room.

Paul was so excited to see his father thinking he could go check the cow herd. Paul yelled, "Me ready, me ready to go to see baby calves," in a little boy's voice, in perfect German.

Henry stood looking and listening to his son but not believing what he had just heard.

Immediately Henry heard Inga say, "No Paul. No, you speak English."

Henry did not say a word. He picked up his son and daughter Margaret and walked to the kitchen. Inga understood Rose's children were to speak English first. His third child Myra, was not awake yet, but her clothes had been laid out by her mother the night before. Henry, Inga and the children had planned a trip to the library and later a picnic.

Rose had many books she brought to Oklahoma when her father had sent her here about eight years ago but they were books the children could read when they grew up.

Henry stood up and greeted Rose as she came into the kitchen. He put his arms around her and kissed her warmly. Her body was large with their new unborn baby. She sat at the table and tried to eat while knowing it would be soon when her labor would start.

Rose had thought this out carefully, not wanting to stop the children's trip today. The children loved going to the library. Her plan was to have Frank, Jay, or William take her to the hospital and on the way she would stop and tell Blue Sky.

After kissing their mother goodby then being lifted into the back of the buggy with Inga, Henry drove Rose's magnificent horse toward the Higgin's Library.

Rose was aware of what was happening within her body but she also felt she had many hours to go before her delivery. She sat at an open window feeling a cool breeze on her face. She could hear some cowhands outside as they rode by the cabin. It was late in the afternoon when things began to change. She suddenly felt a surge of pains coming, one after the other. Rose heard a small tap on the cabin door and her hope was it would be Frank, Jay, or William coming to check on her. Instead, Rose opened the door and Katy was standing there smiling.

Before Rose could say anything, Katy asked her to come to her birthday party at the bunkhouse.

"Oh, Katy," Rose said in a desperate voice. "You must get me some help. See if Frank can take me to the hospital."

"Why? Are you sick?" Katy said in a child's voice.

Katy was tall for her age. Her hair was long, never had it been cut. It hung down to her waist. Her eyes were dark, and her face was beautiful.

"No Katy. You don't understand; my baby is coming." Rose's voice was getting louder. Rose bent over knowing she would not make it to the hospital. "Katy, you must go now and get Blue Sky. Hurry, Katy. Tell one of the cowhands I need help."

"You don't need help," Katy replied calmly. "I can help you."

"No, no, Katy."

"Rose," Katy said. "Go to your room and lie down. Do you have some extra towels?" Katy continued. "I told you I delivered three of the last babies in our family. I can do this."

There was nothing Rose could do but do what Katy told her. She lay in her bed, and Katy came in with a pan of water and several towels. Katy calmly wet a cloth and wiped Rose's face. She then lifted the bottom of the sheet so she could check the progress Rose's baby was making.

"The baby will be born soon but do not push until I tell you to." Katy said it like a grown-up woman, not a ten year old girl.

Rose's hands were white from squeezing the rags Katy had rolled up and placed in each of her hands. Katy continued to wipe Rose's face and gently pushed her hair away from her face. All the while Katy was humming.

"Katy, you need a sharp knife." Before, Rose could finish she had so much pain, she could not finish her sentence.

"Rose, what father taught me to do was tie a string or a piece of thin rag around the cord," said Katy "Do you have a string?"

"Yes. Yes," Rose said breathlessly in between pains saying, "the string is in a drawer next to the stove."

Katy said, in a firm voice, "Push Rose, push. Don't breathe, hold your breath, hold your breath and push."

Rose was so worried, not only about herself but more about her baby.

It happened so fast. Then Rose heard Katy.

Katy's voice sounded so happy when she said, "It's a boy, Rose. You, have a boy. I'm cleaning him off and tying the cord."

Katy lifted the baby into Rose's arms after wrapping him in a towel. Rose looked into the eyes of a perfect baby.

Rose began to laugh with tears rolling down her cheeks. Katy wiped Rose's face with a clean cloth. Rose reached up and pulled Katy to her and kissed her cheek and said, "Thank you, Katy. Thank you."

Katy's reply was, "I told you I could do it."

"Cook made a cake for me. I'll bring you some. I'm ten years old now." Katy sounded like she was celebrating her twentieth birthday.

Rose lay in her bed, holding her new son and thought about the Indian baby she had delivered but she'd been seventeen. Katy was only ten years old. Rose knew Katy was special and she also knew she would take care of her and make sure she got an education. Maybe someday she would be a doctor.

Rose was sure Katy would meet Blue Sky when the news got out.

Chapter 18

Henry entered the cabin first and Katy greeted him with the news. The excitement at the Rose Donlin Helgens' homestead was felt by everyone. The cake Cook made was delicious and everyone came into the cabin to see Henry and Rose's new son.

Henry proudly announced the name that Rose had chosen if the baby was a boy. Joseph Higgins Helgens.

He had given her everything he had. She honored him with the Higgins' Hospital, the Higgins' Library and now her son would carry his name. Rose had so much to tell her children. Joseph Higgins' memory would live on in Oklahoma forever, she would make sure. She would make this son with Joseph's name the governor some day. Then she closed her eyes and went to sleep beside her sleeping son.

Chapter 19

The Higgins' Hospital had prepared a room for Rose Donlin Helgens in preparation for the birth of her baby. A room had been readied for the baby, too.

When the news reached the hospital, everyone was relieved to hear the birth went well, especially the news about Katy delivering Henry and Rose's baby.

Blue Sky entered the hospital quietly as she always did and was greeted by the excited nursing workers. They all talked at the same time. Blue Sky had a concerned look at first, then, she looked sad because she had looked forward to delivering Rose's baby. Blue Sky had made sure Rose's hospital room was ready. She had her bag packed at home. Also, any roots needed for numbness to mix. Her wand was ready to chase any evil spirits away from Rose and her baby. Her prayer beads always hung around her neck.

Without saying a word, Blue Sky left the nurses still standing in the hall talking about the very young girl that had delivered Rose's baby with a perfect procedure.

When Blue Sky arrived at the Helgens' homestead, Rose was sitting up in the rocking chair that Joseph's father had made when his mother announced a baby was on the way many years before. Rose loved the rocking chair because each time she sat in it, her thoughts turned to Joseph Higgins.

Blue Sky tapped lightly on Rose's door, then turned the latch and stepped in so quietly no one heard her.

She whispered, "Rose." Inga was only a couple feet away in the kitchen and did not hear Blue Sky enter.

The first sight Inga had of Blue Sky she threw her arms up in the air and opened her mouth wide to scream. Then realizing it was Blue Sky, stopped with a panic look on her face.

Blue Sky motioned for her to put her arms down, close her mouth and tell Rose she was there. Inga walked to Rose, and all she could do was point.

Blue Sky was dressed in her best Indian attire, and she looked beautiful. Blue Sky kneeled down in front of Rose and reached for baby Joseph. She took the baby to the window the sun was shining in. She held him high above her head and asked her God to bless Joseph and make him a great man.

Later, Blue Sky mentioned how eager she was to meet Katy. Her feelings were a little bitter. Katy, on the other hand, was as happy as any a young girl could be.

Rose sent Inga to get Katy from the bunkhouse.

Katy came into Rose's cabin with a big smile on her face and loving everyone. Blue Sky watched Rose smile at Katy. Katy looked up, saw Blue Sky and could do nothing but stare.

Katy was everything Blue Sky had heard about her, tall for her age, beautiful, long dark hair. Her face was perfect.

Without any warning, Katy took a few giant steps and threw her arms around Blue Sky. The hug was the strength of a young man. Katy had learned to defend herself, being raised with four brothers.

Katy excitedly said, "I want to be just like you."

Blue Sky hesitated, then raised her arms and encircled Katy's tiny waist. This was a moment of peace and contentment.

Blue Sky opened her arms, heart and her home to Katy.

Katy begged to dress like her. She wanted to be an Indian. After Katy's visit to Blue Sky's home, she dressed in Indian attire. Katy did not have a pair of shoes but now she wore only moccasins and was never without feathers in her hair.

Chapter 20

The cowhands were getting more agitated each day and more hostile with each other at night. The barn floor was extremely cold.

Henry explained to Rose they needed to get the squatter family out of the bunkhouse or something bad would happen. Cook appreciated the help from Henry and Berta but the noise made it impossible for him to think, and he wanted peace and quiet.

After the evening meal was finished and cleanup done, Cook walked alone as he did each night. It was just by chance he saw someone off in a distance walking alone. He wondered if they liked being alone as he did.

The days went fast for him. Cowhands came in at all hours for food and lots of coffee. They ate on the run most of the day.

Rufus George had a hard time walking so William came to the kitchen for the meals for all of the men to take back to the oil wells. Cook never admitted to anyone how happy he was to see William each day. William came into the kitchen smiling and always greeted Cook warmly. But, he also teased Cook and always moved the pots around on the stove while Cook was busy and his back was turned.

After the first week, Cook expected William to do it. William laughed easily and forced Cook to smile.

The evening was warm, and Cook started on his usual walk and without being aware he began looking for the person he had seen several times before.

Cook was in his second mile when again he saw the person. He enjoyed watching the person walk and he didn't know why. He just wanted to get closer. It appeared to him the person was walking faster away from him this evening.

Chapter 21

Henry slipped his arms easily around Rose's slender body. Henry's body leaned against her. Joseph was two weeks old now.

Rose listened intently to Henry as he tried to be calm and explain how important it was to find a new home for Harry, Berta and their ten children but close enough, because Cook needed help. The boys were now helping. Rose realized by the tone of Henry's voice, this was urgent.

Rose thought first of Maude. Maude had moved in with Mary, Toby and their family. After Mary's Hank had gotten ill, Mary and Toby had married. Even though Toby was not Maude's real son, she considered him as her own son. Mary also loved Maude. Mary knew Maude would help care for Elizabeth, Sarah and Hank. Mary had secretly told Toby of the wonderful gift they were going to receive in the fall since their marriage a year ago.

Toby and Mary's cabin was large and Maude had her own room in the back portion of the new cabin. Maude had gladly locked up her cabin when Toby invited Maude to come and live with him and Mary.

Rose decided to let Henry take their offer of money to Maude.

The cabin was located close enough for the family of Harry and Berta to walk to the Donlin Helgens' homestead.

The discussion between Henry and Rose making a generous offer to Maude ended and if she accepted, the cabin would be made twice as large for Harry's family.

Henry wasted no time getting Rose's magnificent horse saddled and asking his brother, Frank, to ride along.

The amount offered was so much more than Maude ever would have dreamed of getting for her cabin and ten acres.

Maude accepted the good offer.

Every cowhand available was at Maude's cabin that very afternoon, and the new rooms were started.

Chapter 22

Cook was preparing for his monthly trip into Oklahoma City and to the General Mercantile. Walter, the eldest of Harry's children, wanted to go along. He begged, saying he would help Cook load the wagon, which was always full. Cook thought it over carefully, even though he wanted to be alone.

When Cook finally agreed to let Walter go, the other three boys began to make a scene, asking why they couldn't go. They would ride any horse available. They also begged and promised to help load the wagon.

Cook was busy preparing his list. Checking the shelves and writing down his important needs. He did not see the horses the boys picked out to saddle up. The one horse Cook did not see until the boys dismounted in Oklahoma in front of the mercantile. His mouth opened to holler and nothing came out. The shock on his face of what he was looking at and the young man, Walter had no concern of what he had done.

He was sitting on top of Roses' magnificent giant horse.

Cook's first thought was to turn and take all of the boys and go right back to the bunkhouse. His second thought was they were all in trouble already, so his thought was to load up as fast as he could and get right back.

Everything seemed to be going well; the wagon was filling up fast. The boys were carrying the boxes one after another.

Then Cook noticed the letters on one of the boxes as it passed him being carried by as fast as Walter could carry it.

In big black letters it spelled 'Licorice.' The next boy was carrying a box with the letters "Hard Sugar Candy."

Cook's loud voice yelled, "Stop." The boys stopped.

Then Cook yelled, "Set the boxes down." The boys stopped but refused to set the boxes down.

Walter spoke first saying, "The boxes are for our brothers and sisters, not us."

Cook thought back when he was a boy and his father brought a licorice home for him. Cook did not say another word but waved his arm in the direction of the wagon. With no hesitation the boys hurried out the door and placed the boxes in the wagon next to the two other boxes with the same letters.

Cook yelled for the boys to mount up. He was distracted and feeling agitated as he ordered the boys to start back to Rose's homestead. He crawled up on the buckboard seat and glanced back of the wagon so he didn't pull out in front of anyone. As his eyes took in the street and sidewalk, he turned to take another look at an elderly man. Cook stopped the horses and looked again. He could see only his back when the man opened the door into the bank and walked out of sight.

Cook wanted to jump down and follow the man into the bank but he heard the boys holler at him.

The ride back was as fast as the wagon could travel. No one paid any attention as Cook and the food wagon pulled up to the kitchen at the end of the bunkhouse.

No one, but Rose Donlin Helgens'. She watched as her horse walked behind the food wagon, and riding on the back of her horse was Walter.

Walter was riding bareback. Rose knew it was because of her giant horse's height. He could not get the saddle on him.

No one had ever ridden on her horse or had been permitted to ride her horse except Henry or Frank with her permission.

Walter climbed down off of the giant horse without knowing he was being watched. He talked softly to the horse and patted him. Walter patted the side of the horse's head. He reached around with his arms up as high as he could to hug the giant horse but could not come close to the top of his head. Rose watched silently while Walter hugged and kissed her horse.

This was not what Rose had imagined she would see. Walter had never had one thing of his own. He was born into poverty and his role in the big family was being in charge, in a loving way, yet he was defiant to society. His fourteen years was always struggling to help his family, to prove his family was as good as other families. The tricks he played on others gave him a sense of right, making him feel equal.

Rose was watching a part of Walter no one else knew existed. He loved Rose's horse.

"Walter," Rose said his name clearly and precise. Walter jumped from not knowing anyone was there in the large barn Rose's horse was stalled in. He took a couple steps to run and Rose said his name again and then said, "Stop." Walter stopped and stood with his back to her.

"Walter, my horse is my horse. Do you understand that?"

His head went down and in a whisper, Walter said, "Yes, I know that."

"I would like you to rub him down after I ride him. Would you do that for me?" Rose asked in a soft kind voice.

Yes, I can do that," Walter answered with a smile on his face.

"I also have something you might like" Rose continued. "One of Henry's mares is ready to foal. You may spend as much time with her as you like. With your parent's permission, the colt will be yours."

Rose heard some sniffling; he was trying so hard not to cry. Walter could only nod his head. Rose turned and left the barn, leaving Walter to cry in happiness by himself.

Chapter 23

Dora had spent the day in the big white house baking bread and making cookies. She had not gotten used to being alone. Going to bed early seemed the only thing for her to do.

When Walter crawled out of the tunnel and into the fruit room he could smell the good aroma of homemade bread, and the cookies' smell always made him hungry.

He had one thing on his mind, getting upstairs and eating bread and cookies. He didn't stop at one slice of bread, he took one entire loaf. The cookies were on two plates covered with a kitchen towel. He took one plate full of cookies. Wilber returned to the basement and then on into the tunnel.

He tore pieces off of the bread and within a half an hour he had eaten the whole loaf of bread. The cookies were so good, just like Dora always made. He ate one cookie after another until the plate was clean. Then he lay down on his quilt in the tunnel, rubbed his stomach, and went to sleep.

Wilber woke knowing he had to hurry, morning was near. Crawling through the tunnel as fast as he could, then out through the barn and straight for the Kolveck settlement. He needed more supplies.

He needed more pails to carry dirt out of his tunnel. His lantern needed kerosene. He also thought he needed a bigger package of hard candy.

The general store was getting harder for him to get into as new locks were put on after Wilber broke in each time. He filled one pail with candy sticks from the glass jars sitting on the counter. Cookies were coming in packages now. He filled the other pail with cookie packages. The can of kerosene was hard to carry, walking slowly he got home just at dawn.

Dora's visitor knocked on the big white, house door early before Dora had discovered her missing food.

Opening the door brought mixed feelings. She felt guilty, and also very happy to see Rose Donlin Helgens' again.

"Dora, may I come in?" Rose's voice sounded pleasant.

"Yes, Yes, of course. Please come in and have coffee." Dora needed someone to talk to as her life was empty and lonely.

Rose could see no change in the rooms since she had been there. It made her feel a little uneasy at first just being there.

Dora quickly made the coffee and took the towel off of the cookies. She suddenly expressed her surprise about one plate of cookies missing and then finding one loaf of bread missing.

"Was someone else in your house Dora?" Rose asked in a whisper as if she thought someone was listening.

"No, no. Only me," Dora answered back in a raspy whisper.

Rose did not like it that Dora was alone in the big white house.

"Dora, would you mind if Henry's brothers come and look around for you? Maybe you need new bolts on your doors," said Rose.

"Please ask them to come," Dora answered.

Chapter 24

Frank continued to care for the mare after she had dropped her foal with Walter sleeping with the Mare and her foal. Frank thought it was time for the mare and her over active foal to go outside in the yard. Walter's excitement was unmanageable. He told his parents, siblings and any cowhand who would listen.

The mare stepped out first and behind her with one giant leap and falling on his nose, the colt was greeted with cheers from Harry and Berta and all of their children. All of the cowhands working on the homestead, Henry, Rose, Inga, Paul showed as much enthusiasm as Walter. Margaret, Myra and Joseph wrapped up in blankets in Rose's arms.

The colt was perfect. He jumped, first kicking his front legs up as high as he could, then kicking his back legs in the air. He ran around his mother; then he ran under his mother. Everyone clapped, yelled and laughed. He was beautiful. He ran toward the fence where Rose was standing. He stopped and looked at her, and Paul reached for him and giggled with happiness.

Rose studied the colt and the thought crossed her mind if this beautiful foal of Henry's mare could possibly belong to her magnificent horse. She decided to mention it to both Henry and Frank.

Frank directed Walter to climb down off of the fence and into the yard. Everyone watched knowing how much Walter loved his new prized colt. Frank was standing next to Walter, and in his hand was a halter he had made especially with shiny silver beads.

Frank motioned for William, Jay and Thomas. The men cornered the colt. It took them all to hold him while Walter put the new halter on him. No noise was heard until the men all stepped back and the colt leaped in the air and started running and bucking. He had everyone's attention.

It would take time and patience but Walter would train the colt.

Chapter 25

The train came to a stop and Mr. and Mrs. Morrison and their son stepped down off of the train in Oklahoma City. The Morrison family lost their daughter two years ago on the same night Mary gave birth to her son. One baby died while the other went home with Mary. The Morrison family is mourning and cannot come to believe the loss.

Mrs. Morrison was carrying a large looking book. Blue Sky greeted them warmly, noticing the book of pictures. The Morrison family had sent word to Rose they were coming to help celebrate Hank's second birthday. Mary was expecting the birth of Toby's baby so for several reasons Blue Sky offered to get the Morrison family and take them to the boarding house where she had ordered rooms for two days.

The first place Mrs. Morrison wanted to take her family was to the grave site of their daughter and sister. It was here she sat down and showed Blue Sky all of the pictures of her daughter who had given birth to a boy. Both had died in the Higgins' Hospital on that stormy night two years before.

She showed pictures of Ruby Morrison as a baby, child and adult. Blue Sky looked and studied all of the pictures without saying a word. Blue Sky had seen Hank frequently because of caring for Mary. The pictures told and expressed so many things but no words would ever be said.

Hank looked exactly like his real mother.

Mrs. Morrison then asked to go to the hospital after leaving the cemetery. Blue Sky did not argue. She drove the buggy up to the front door.

Mrs. Morrison questioned each nurse on duty as she had done before, asking if they were working that night her daughter gave birth and died. One nurse remembered she was. She talked to Mrs. Morrison privately.

Blue Sky was concerned but not worried. She and Rose had taken care of every detail that night. No one was allowed in the two rooms. One room was where Ruby was with Mary's son. One room was where Ruby's live baby was.

Only Rose and Blue Sky knew the secret.

At Hank's second birthday celebration, Mrs. Morrison made sure everyone looked at the album. Mr. Morrison cried when he saw Hank. Ruby's brother begged to hold him.

Rose asked Blue Sky to spend every moment with the Morrison family as she had done before and to make sure Mrs. Morrison did not take Hank on the train with her.

Mrs. Morrison announced at the birthday party her gift to Hank was a portrait of him and his family. She had made the appointment for the next day.

When the picture of Hank's family was completed, Mrs. Morrison insisted Hank have a picture taken by himself.

Blue Sky wanted to stop her but did not want to make a scene. Blue Sky heard Mrs. Morrison asked the photographer when he would have the picture done, and instructed him to send it to her.

The photographer explained it would take a few days but he would send all of the pictures to her.

Blue Sky contemplated intercepting the pictures and destroying them because she was sure Mrs. Morrison wanted to compare the new picture with the ones she had of her daughter.

It was so sad but Mrs. Morrison had no proof. A secret is a secret.

Chapter 26

Cook hurried to get the last cowhands fed, and the kitchen cleaned up. It had been warm all day and with the big iron stove heated up, the kitchen was especially hot. His mind was on starting a cool evening walk and being alone. No one paid any attention because he did not talk to any of the cowhands.

He went to the pump first and washed his arms and face along with his long hair. He was feeling anguish, hoping he would see the person he had seen before. Then he started on his walk.

He had walked nearly three miles and then he saw a figure off in the distance like he had seen before. Then just within a few minutes, the person disappeared.

Cook decided to slow down. He didn't think he would see the person again this night.

He did not hear any noise behind him until he heard a voice say, "Are you following me?"

Cook turned around to look into the most beautiful dark brown eyes he had ever seen. Her hair was black and hanging loosely to her waist. She had skin of soft brown. Her brown buckskin vest and skirt fit on a tall, thin Indian woman. Her leather boots came up to her knees.

She had circled around him without his knowing she was there before she spoke.

"No. Yes, no. I wasn't following you exactly," Cook tried to explain. "I've seen you when I have been out walking. I did wonder who you were."

A slight smile appeared on her lips when she said," My name is Blue Sky."

"Everyone calls me Cook, my real name is Albert. I work for Rose Donlin Helgens."

"I'm happy to meet you Cook, but I will call you Albert," Blue Sky said as she extended her hand.

Albert reached out slowly and took her hand in both of his and whispered, "I'm so happy to meet you, Blue Sky."

This was totally different for a man with no friends, and no one to talk to. No one ever talked to him.

Albert looked down at the ground and said, "Could we meet here tomorrow night?"

Blue Sky reached over and lifted his chin up and looked into his eyes, saying, "Yes, I'll be here. You must not tell anyone."

Cook simply nodded. Cook had never felt this good before. Not since being a boy. It was such a different good.

The following day was busy for Cook but at no time did he not think about meeting the most beautiful Indian woman.

Blue Sky was a little late getting to the place where they were to meet. She found Cook sitting on the ground waiting. He did not hear her until she sat down next to him.

Albert's voice was a little shaky when he said, "I was afraid you would not come."

The sad look on his face made her realize she had to reassure him that she always told the truth. Blue Sky saw something on his face and heard something in his voice she had never witnessed from a white man before.

After meeting every night for many nights Blue Sky needed to tell him they could only be friends. They could never marry.

The evenings were getting cooler and she asked Albert if he would like to come to her cabin but to be very careful not to be seen.

The night finally arrived. He approached the cabin after dark and stood in the shadows making sure he was not seen.

Blue Sky opened the back door to let him into a dark cabin. She stepped close to him, shutting the door behind him. Their bodies touched, and they stood in the dark feeling each other's body. Her arms circled his neck and he pulled her even closer. Their cheeks came together and in the dark cabin they shared their first kiss.

When Albert left the cabin that night, he knew he would never give her up. He had found what he had lost when his mother died and his father left him so many years ago, love. But this love was between a man and a woman.

Chapter 27

Blue Sky needed to tell him how badly white men were treated when they chose to marry an Indian woman. She knew if she married him, she would be called a white man's squaw. That was something she would not consent to, no matter how much she loved him. Also, Albert would be treated badly, and Blue Sky did not want this to happen to one of the nicest and kindness man she had ever met.

She needed to tell him about the hurtful feeling he would have when they met on the street in Oklahoma City or in the general store when he made his monthly trip for food supplies.

Before Blue Sky had this conversation with Albert, it happened. It happened the next morning after they had spent a wonderful evening sharing their love. Albert was standing in the general store, checking his food list.

Blue Sky walked in with Rose. Albert wanted to walk up to her to show the feeling of love he had for Blue Sky. Albert took a couple steps towards her. Suddenly Rose stepped between them and said his name.

Blue Sky walked away without a glance in his direction. She was right. He was so hurt. Hurt and disappointed.

He tried to stay away. He didn't go on his usual walk the next few evenings. He was in love with Blue Sky and he didn't care who knew it.

Rose Donlin Helgens' stepped into the kitchen when Cook was finishing cleaning up after the last cowhands had been fed and the large amount of pancake mix was placed in the new ice box for breakfast.

"Albert," Rose said. "Blue Sky and I keep no secrets between us. I know how you feel about her. But you must understand how you would hurt her if anyone should find out. She would not fit into her Indian family and she would never fit into the white man's world. If you love her you will love her from afar with your meetings on walks and in her cabin."

"Rose, I can't do that. I love her too much," Cook said with his teeth clinched.

Albert had lived through the loss of two people he had loved from the beginning of his life. Now he was finding the pain too much to bear.

"Albert, I'm going to help you both," said Rose "I have a wonderful place; it is located by my private inlet at Joseph's. I'm going to build a secret cabin for you both to meet. No one will know it's for you and Blue Sky."

Chapter 28

Frank, Jay, William and Thomas rode off from the Rose Donlin Helgens' homestead, heading to the big white house.

Wilber had been busy as soon as the sun went down and the night time darkness arrived.

He crawled through the tunnel in his usual speed and paid no attention to the small pieces of dirt falling on him. He had seen something in the general store he wanted but could not carry it with so many other things he had to carry the night before.

The front door of the general store was locked he was sure. He stayed in the dark alley.

It wasn't the general store he would enter. It was the building next to the general store. The stores were all connected so his entrance was into the boarding house. He had not taken anything, so the authorities did not know he went through the boarding house to get to the general store.

The door between the buildings was not locked. He took his usual route, crawling under the boarding house and then pushing open the cave door up into the boarding house's back storage room.

He tried to be very quiet so he would not awaken anyone sleeping in the boarding house. Wilber slipped into the general store and went right toward the gun area. First, he looked at the rifles hanging on the wall and then spotted the pistol he wanted so badly. Next, he had to find the bullets to fit his new gun.

His father was a hunter but he would never take Wilber with him, he would always take Dora. Wilber remembered how he felt when his father said, "NO. You can't go hunting. You're too dumb to hold or shoot a gun."

Now Wilber would show everyone, he had his own gun.

When he was ready to leave, he looked up and saw a hunting knife. Memories flooded back to him about his father always carrying a hunting knife. He wanted the knife.

Wilber slipped the knife into his belt buckle. He felt so good and proud. He was now a hunter.

He reached the big white house while it was dark. Crawling through the tunnel was never easy. While he was crawling, it stirred up dust and made it difficult to breath. As soon as he was at the end of the tunnel, he pushed the trunk so a little fresh air would help him breath.

Once he felt better breathing, he crawled a few feet back into the tunnel wrapped up into his quilt and went to sleep for the day.

Henry's brothers rode into the Kolveck settlement. People on the street could not help but stare as strangers were noticed immediately; everyone in Kolveck settlement knew each other.

The brothers walked in pairs all over the settlement, and also down each alley because the general store was the only store merchandise was missing. They examined carefully all of the entrances into the store. Nothing showed up.

Each brother tried to talk to the people on the street. No one would talk to the brothers. The ones that would talk only wanted to talk about how strange a person Wilber was, how he never had to work, how Dora always took care of him. The brother's rode home feeling disappointed.

Chapter 29

Rose mentioned building a small summer cabin for their family. The children could swim and play along the water. Henry was excited about a cabin near the water for his family. The lumber would be ordered and any cowhand not busy would be informed of building the cabin immediately. Rose also mentioned the cabin was to be called "Higgins' Private Cabin."

The cabin would fit in between trees so no trees would have to be removed. Rose ordered the cabin to be made strong and safe. No animals would get in. Not like the cabin she had lived in when she first came here. A large porch would be built looking out over the clear blue water. The view of the wild flowers, pink, yellow and blue along the bank could be seen from the porch, too. The cool breeze would be felt while sitting on the porch any evening.

Rose ordered straw mattresses to lie all along one wall. The wall was not to have any windows in it.

The fireplace was to be located on the wall next to the mattresses. A secret cupboard would be built for wine bottles.

The pantry would be filled with food to cook over the fireplace. Rose ordered a table and chairs from the mercantile, along with lamps. The window curtains would be made with colorful feed sack material. No one could see in any window. The steel lock on the door would stop intruders.

Rose asked William to row the canoe up to the new cabin. It was the same canoe Rose took Joseph on several rides. At first, he was very reluctant to get in the canoe, but after the first trip he didn't want it to stop.

Albert and Blue Sky would be able to go on only short trips because of the fear of being seen.

The culture would not change for a very long time. Blue Sky's Indian heritage was her way of life. Nothing in her life would change except the happiness she felt being in love with Albert.

Chapter 30

Cook insisted no one go with him on his trip into the general store to purchase the month's supply of food for the Helgens' homestead. He had been thinking about the man he had seen on the trip when Walter rode on Rose's giant horse.

He needed time to walk around and ask about the man he had seen.

Cook started by asking the clerk in the general store. The clerk told him to go to the stable, "Sometimes" he said," men ride in and leave their horses for a few weeks to rest and drink or they come looking for a job." Turning around and walking to the backyard, the stableman pointed toward the horse. Cook recognized immediately the horse was the one his father rode away with when he left their home so abruptly. But how did he end up here? Cook was overwhelmed.

"Is this the one? Are you going to pay me now?" asked the stableman, becoming irritated over Cook's slow reaction.

"I don't care about the horse. It's the man I want to see," Cook replied indignantly. "I need the money," the stableman said raising his voice. "That nag has eaten more hay than any other horse in the stable."

"First," Cook said, while holding up his hand and pointing his finger directly at the stableman. Lowering his voice, Cook said, "You send the owner of this horse to the Rose Donlin Helgens' homestead, and I'll pay the bill."

The two men stood looking at each other with total dislike for the other. Neither spoke again. Cook left to return to the mercantile and his wagon of food. He hurried the team back to the bunkhouse kitchen, afraid he would be late for his evening walk. He unloaded the boxes in the right order each box placed for easy access.

The evening meal was over, and the cleaning done. Walter never stopped talking to all the cowhands while they ate. He kept them all informed about the progress of taming his prized colt. Any information he got from men who were experts he used.

Katy and her sister Abigail, offered to help at the noon and evening meal. The girls were learning to bake cookies and pie. The men ate anything they baked after a good meal made by Cook.

Cook's walk was fast as he headed for Blue Sky's cabin, now that it was dark. He stepped in without knocking. Blue Sky reached out touching him as soon as he closed the door. Nothing else mattered now he was holding the love of his life in his arms. Her body felt so good to him. She was soft and warm. Her breasts were pressed against his chest.

He wanted to tell the world how he felt about this beautiful Indian woman, but he knew if he were to keep her, this would be their life together. Never seen together; always alone; hiding their love.

Cook arrived back at the bunkhouse in time to start breakfast.

It was late in the afternoon when Harry told Cook a man was outside asking to talk to Albert. Cook's breath caught in his throat, making him cough as he stepped out of the door into the sunshine, thinking he was going to see his father. No one here but Blue Sky knew his real name. Cook tried hard not to show his disappointment. The first glance he knew the man riding his father's horse was not his father.

"Where did you get that horse?" Cook said angrily, trying to mask his pain.

"I bought him off of a man down on his luck somewhere in Kansas," The stranger said. "He told me a story about his wife dying in a flu epidemic. And he also talked about a son he left behind. Of course, he was drunk."

"No, no, not my father. It must have been someone else who stole his horse," said Cook.

"Oh yeah; One more thing he told me, he dug a sod house for his wife. He said it was located in South Dakota."

"Get the hell off of this property now!" Cook yelled.

"I thought you'd help me pay my horse's feed bill," the man said while moving his horse to leave knowing how mad Cook was. Cook did not want to hear another word from this man. He also did not want to believe what the man had said.

As much as Cook wanted to deny it, everything the man said was true. It was hard to believe his father was drinking. He had always told Albert how bad it was for a man to turn to drink for comfort.

Suddenly the old feeling overwhelmed him. The loneliness he had felt when he realized at age fifteen, he was all alone.

He did promise his mother he would find his father. So, he would keep looking.

Chapter 31

Rose greeted Henry's brothers asking about what they had found. Frank was first to speak, telling Rose how the people of the Kolveck settlement would not talk to them, only about Wilber's strange life.

Jay was determined to go back. He told Rose, "I can't understand how Wilber could get into the general store. The doors were locked tight on the inside and outside of the front door and the only door entering through the back alley was bolted shut. He enters somewhere else."

Jay said, "We need to go back and wait for him. But we need to go after it gets dark" "I think you're right," Frank said, "We'll go tonight."

William told Rose, "We need to go back to the house and start over. He has to be leaving the house from somewhere but we just haven't found it yet."

"Rose," Frank said, "Tell Henry we'll be in the bunkhouse sleeping this afternoon because we'll be up all night searching again for Wilber."

Frank was ready. First he ate and talked with Cook about his helpers. Cook was quick to defend the girls, Katy and Abigail, for their constant improvement in pie and cookie baking.

Jay came into the kitchen to see what he could find to eat; walking in behind him was William. William was singing to himself as he picked up a hand-full of cookies. Stuffing them all in his mouth, then smiling at Cook with the cookies showing in his mouth.

Cook couldn't get mad. He liked William so he smiled back while moving the cookies out of Williams reach.

The brothers ate and discussed how they should catch Wilber at night. They were sure Wilber came out at night. He was never seen during the day. The three brothers rode in the dark without talking.

Frank took his position next to the cave door leading into the basement. This was the door Wilber had entered the big white house when he snuck back into the house. Jay was watching the door for anyone coming out of the house from behind a tree in the backyard. This door was the door Wilber and Dora took Henry into when they had pulled him from the raging creek and kept him there prisoner for seven months. Jay slid down the tree and sat on the ground. He looked up in the sky and a million shining stars looked down at him. He wondered how one unstable man could be so clever.

William was looking at the front of the house. They all felt confident of catching Wilber. He couldn't slip away or get back into the house. The brothers were all ready. No one would get by them.

The night was long, and the noises were loud at times. Crickets were chirping. Off in the distant an owl hooted. Frogs from the near- by creek were croaking to each other.

While the brothers were all around the house, Wilber was crawling through the underground tunnel and out through the hole in the manger of the barn. He had no problem getting into town and into the general store.

Wilber liked the new packaged cookies and candy. He also picked up a pair of pants and a shirt he thought would fit him.

The shelves of fruit looked good but carrying so much would be hard. He was using so many of Dora's fruit jars, holding two was all he could carry.

Wilber had noticed the horses behind the barn when he left. He could see their outline and heard their noises when he came back. He thought about turning the horses loose but if they made a lot of noise whoever was looking for him would hear their horses so he quickly went into the tunnel and safety.

The first light of the morning came, and the three brothers had seen no one. They gathered at their horses tied behind Dora's barn. It was beginning to get cold, and they huddled together talking about what they would do next.

Frank suggested before they rode home they should ride into the Kolveck settlement and ask if there were any more break-ins.

The store clerk at the general store was up early to discover several things missing again. The doors were not broken into, and he was furious that no one could stop the person doing it. Frank, Jay and William explained what they had done the night before and were beginning to think it could be someone else other than Wilber.

While the men were talking, William walked out into the back alley behind the general store. He looked at the lock on the back door, and it had not been tampered with. He examined every window and then walked a little farther to the boarding house. Then he saw a door with the lock broken. He pried open the door and found he was in the back room of the boarding house. He pushed open an unlocked door and got down on his knees to crawl through a crawl space. Then he lifted the door up over his head climbing into the boarding house, closed the door as he looked around in the boarding house, he could hear the men talking in the general store.

William walked into the general store where the rooms were connected.

The men looked up with shock and surprise on their face's as William walked in grinning. He had found how Wilber got in and out of the locked and bolted doors of the general exchange store. Now, all the men had to do was find the one guilty of the stealing.

Chapter 32

Albert arrived first at the new Joseph Higgins' Private Cabin for their night of discovery. He found the secret cupboard of wine. He prepared food in the big black kettle hanging over the fireplace. He brought along two pieces of pie Katy had made for the cowhands dessert that night. The table was set and ready for Blue Sky when she arrived. Albert did not hear her enter the cabin. Blue Sky was wearing her soft high top leather boots. She made no noise at all. The boots were hand made by an old Indian man in her tribe. They were laced up with blue and white beads. She was wearing her white Indian attire and looked beautiful with her long black hair hanging to her waist. She had a small hand full of white feathers on one side of her head.

Albert turned and smiled as he took her small hand in his and helped her into their new home. He pulled her chair out from the table and politely asked her to sit down while he filled her plate. Katy's pie was delicious.

Even the birds were happy filling the trees surrounding the cabin. The water flowing in the creek made little splashing sounds.

When they had finished eating, Albert reached for her, and they walked to the mattress on the floor.

Albert was on his knees as was Blue Sky. He lifted her left hand up. He removed a ring from his small finger he had been wearing since the death of his mother. He slipped the ring on her third finger and as he did, with tears welling up in his eyes, said, "You are my love, Blue Sky. I give you my promise to be the best husband and man I can be. I will never leave you no matter what."

"I will wear this ring the rest of my life while loving you as my husband," said Blue Sky with tears falling down her beautiful face. "The division of my people will never stop me from my love for you."

Albert had made arrangements for the squatter family to do all of the meals the next day. No one knew what he was doing or where he was going. He had refused to tell anyone.

The night turned into a day of happiness. It started with a canoe ride. The beauty of their surroundings and their love for each other was all they wanted. They could only go so far and then they would reverse their paddles to return to the cabin.

Rose had mentioned to Blue Sky how warm the water was in her former private inlet. Albert and Blue Sky both knew how to swim in any type of water. The inlet water was calm and with no swimming suits made their swimming fun time perfect.

Then later Albert wanted to share all of his secrets he had never told anyone. Even the small ones, the one that is still hurting.

Blue Sky listened without saying a word until he was done. Then she said, "Maybe I can help. I have some very good friends in Oklahoma City that could look around."

Albert began to be upset and he said, "No, Blue Sky. You must not let anyone know you know me or my story. We do not want people to know we know each other. I understand now how we must live. I could not bear to lose you. I love you too much I will die if I lose you."

Blue Sky moved as close to him as she could and put her arms tightly around him. She tipped her head up and put her lips on his.

She would not interfere.

Chapter 33

Rose woke to hearing Paul begging and pleading. Rose could hear him saying, "See, Baby Nay. See Baby Nay. Please, Mama. Please, Mama." Then he started over repeating his begging. Rose quickly slipped out of bed and hurried down the hall to Paul's room. She greeted him with a hug and many kisses while he kept up his pleading.

"We can go see Walter's colt as soon as we eat breakfast, Paul." Rose said gently but firmly. Rose and Henry's family sat around the large table in the kitchen. The table had been brought up from Joseph's old cabin. The table was large enough for Rose's growing family.

Joseph's father had made the table when Joseph was on the way. Joseph had told Rose her father made the table big hoping to have a large family. But after his baby sister died, they no longer could have another child.

All of Rose's children had their own place at the table. Henry bowed his head and prayed. The children folded their hands as be began to pray. The twins, Paul and Margaret were three years old. Myra was two years. Joseph was close to a year old. Rose sat at the table looking at the family she loved so much. Her children would always have each other, not like she who grew up alone. Without being aware, her hand moved and she laid it on her stomach.

Paul continued to beg to see the new colt. Rose told Paul, "We will all go to the corral as soon as Walter brings him out."

Rose was distracted with Paul's restless outburst. When Paul was finally eating, Rose quickly asked Henry, "Is it possible Walter's new colt is the son of my magnificent horse?" Henry was suddenly deep in thought and finally said, "Rose, the only time it could have happened was the night the horses got out. Frank brought them back and locked them up and he had ridden your horse in with them all. He left your horse in with them while he locked the gate, fed and watered them."

"I remember Frank asking me if I knew if my mare was expecting. Of course, I knew nothing about it," Henry said, knowing it meant more now than it did then. Rose tried not to show her disappointment. If only she had known, the colt would have been saved for Paul.

After breakfast, Henry helped Rose take their family to the corral built for Walter and his colt. The colt was growing fast. His coat was black, and Walter brushed him several times a day. His legs were larger and strong now. He stood many hands higher than any of the other colts born in the Spring. The colt ran around the fence, then stopped and reared up on his back legs. Rose could see the muscles were strong and firm.

Henry and Rose looked at each other, knowing the truth was out. Walter's beautiful colt was a descendent of Rose's magnificent horse.

Rose lovingly watched the colt. She decided a colt for Paul, Joseph and any other son she might have, was needed in the future. Picking out just the right mare would be a big decision for her. Henry had a discussion with Frank about what they had discovered. Frank spent much time looking at the colt. He touched him all over, feeling his firm hard muscles. His bright eyes never missed anything. His mane was thick and long. His chest was broad and muscular.

Frank now agreed the beautiful colt was from Henry's mare and Rose's magnificent horse. Frank felt an obligation to do what Rose had mentioned. He would find a mare to produce the colts Rose wanted for her sons.

Frank took a fast trip into Oklahoma City to look at horses in a sales ring. He checked out all the mares for sale. None would fit into the requirements of mating with Rose's giant horse. Finding the right mare would take time.

Chapter 34

Mary loved carrying Toby's baby. She felt so much love from Toby, so loving his baby was easy. Toby was nothing like Jessie Rocker. Elizabeth and Sarah's memories of their real father were fading. They never talked about him after Toby married their mother.

Mary had left her first husband, Jessie Rocker not knowing she was carrying his son. The baby Mary took home from the hospital only knew Toby as his father. Toby's baby was right on time. Toby nervously hitched his horse to the buggy. He helped Mary up into the seat beside him while Mary continued to give Maude instructions on carrying for Elizabeth, Sarah and Hank.

The day had started out pleasant but by noon clouds had covered the blue sky. The threat of rain was upon them. Lightning was sharp and striking frequently across the sky. Toby wrapped a blanket around Mary to make sure the rain would not get to her.

Mary remembered the ride two years ago with Maude driving her to the hospital. This ride was just like it. Mary hugged her stomach, protecting her baby.

Toby drove the buggy up to the hospital as close as he could get. He hurried her inside finding a nurse and Blue Sky.

Maude loved each of the children. She had cared for the girls as soon as Mary met Toby. After Hank was born, Toby was more determined than ever to marry this beautiful woman with three children. He had fallen deeply in love with Mary and her children.

Blue Sky was at Mary's bedside as she was when Mary's baby boy was born two years ago. The rain was not letting up. The nurse pulled all the curtains closed to keep Mary from seeing the wicked lightning.

Mary could hear Rose's voice coming in from the hall. Rose was asking the nurse what room Mary was in. The nurse directed Rose to Mary, the same room she had had her baby in two years ago. Rose tapped lightly on Mary's door but entered immediately. Blue Sky looked up with a puzzling look on her face. She had Mary ready for delivery. Everything was going well, not like the last baby Mary had.

Toby and Mary's son was born at the same time the storm ended. The clouds vanished and the heaven filled with millions of stars. The room became bright as a full moon made it look like day time. The baby's first cry could be heard all over the hospital. Blue Sky had just blessed him and prayed over him then she took the baby to another room. Rose slipped in and watched as Blue Sky cleaned him up. The two women stood very close to each other looking intently at Mary's new baby. They were trying hard to remember if this baby looked anything like Hank did at birth.

Hank's hair was getting darker and was very curly but it was light when he was born. The baby's hair was light. The baby's skin color appeared lighter than Hank's. Hank's skin color had been light when he was born, but as he grew and after his first birthday his skin color looked darker. The baby's eyes could change in time so both women were not concerned. Hank's eyes had turned very dark.

Blue Sky rewrapped Toby's baby, she and Rose left the room. Rose left for her home feeling insecure. Blue Sky took the baby to his parents. Both Blue Sky and Rose felt the secret was still their secret, but why was Hank so dark?

Blue Sky walked into Mary's room and joyous happiness filled the room. Maude and the girls with Hank came minutes later, each one begging to hold the new baby. No one in the room saw the difference between the sons of Mary, except Blue Sky.

Blue Sky was concerned over not seeing any resemblance between Mary's two sons. Both of Mary's daughters were light skinned and their hair was light brown.

Another concern Blue Sky and Rose had, was the picture Mrs. Morrison would receive in the mail of Hank.

Chapter 35

Rose sat silent listening to Henry's brothers telling her how they could not find Wilber Kolveck. She watched their sober faces and she looked into their dull eyes. They each told her how they watched the big white house all night and no one left the house or entered it.

Then each reported how it was finally discovered how the thief was breaking into the mercantile store.

They shared with Rose an idea of going back to the Kolveck settlement to set a trap to catch Wilber Kolveck or if it turns out not to be Wilber, they stop the person from stealing any more merchandise.

Rose could see how determined they were to go back and try again. She was also pleased when they told her their plan.

Frank said, "I'll be in the alley behind the general store next to the door that leads into the boarding house. He will not get by me."

Jay was next offering to stay next to the big white house. He continued by saying he would walk around the house several times during the night.

"I can walk along the road into the Kolveck settlement and stop anyone on the road after dark." William said, then adding, "I'll walk on foot and leave my horse by Dora's barn."

Each brother left Rose's homestead with a gun in their holster and a rifle on their saddle.

It was after dark so no one saw them leave or no one knew they had left, they would catch Wilber Kolveck this time.

Frank rode his horse straight into town while Jay stopped at the big white house and tied his horse in the front of the barn.

William rode along with Jay and after arriving at the big white house he tied his horse next to Jay's. William left on foot to walk the road that led everyone into the Kolveck settlement. The two horses tied a few feet apart were noisy and restless. Each one was stomping and stepping around.

Wilber dressed for going out. He started through the tunnel and as he reached the opening into the manger he heard horse noises and he knew it wasn't Dora's old team. He stopped and listened. After crawling out of the manger he slipped over to the door far enough to see the outline of two horses. He turned, crawled back into the manger and then on back into the tunnel. Something was happening but he didn't know what.

Wilber crawled to the tunnel opening behind the large old trunk in the fruit room. He pushed the trunk far enough to crawl out into the dark fruit room. He then pushed the big trunk back so no one could see the tunnel opening in case he was seen.

Being as quiet as he could Wilber climbed the stairs into Dora's kitchen. He took what he wanted, cookies and fresh bread. He was sure Dora was asleep upstairs with her door closed.

Then he saw something through one of Dora's windows, he saw the figure of a tall man walking around the house.

Now he knew what was going on. They were looking for him.

He turned and hurried to the basement steps, closing the door behind him, he headed for the tunnel. Wilber pulled the trunk out and then crawled in pulling the trunk as close as he could get it to the fruit room wall.

He sat down and put his head down feeling out of breath but happy about how the game was going. He wondered how Dora had gotten someone else to play in the game.

Wilber did not want to get caught, not yet. He needed to think of another place to hide in. All of the other hiding places had been good but he felt it was time to move.

Wilber lay back on his quilt and tried to rest, thinking of where he could go. He remembered the night he left Rufus George. He thought about all of the young children playing in and near Rose Donlin's bunkhouse.

He overheard someone say they missed the old shanty on Rose's north forty.

The old shanty would be perfect for him. He packed his cookies, candy and bread in one of his pails. He folded up his patch quilt and in the other pail he put his new pants, shirt and socks that he had taken from the mercantile store.

Wilber slept until it was almost dawn, then emerged from the tunnel, closed the tunnel up tight with the big trunk.

Carrying his pails climbed the steps up to the cave door leading outside. As fast as he could go he headed for the wooded creek area where he would stay until it was dark again and then he would sneak toward the Rose Donlin land. He had heard one of the boys say the shanty was north and that's the direction he walked in.

When Wilber got to the wooded area hurrying was impossible. The trees were close together and with weed and dense brush grown up they were all matted together making it horrible for him. He was scratched on his arms and face. It was dark and scary it made him sick to his stomach.

The shrill was high pitched yet it sounded like a grunt, it sent Wilber collapsing to the undergrowth of leaves, twigs and sharp weeds. He dropped his pails and sat with his eyes closed. This was the far-worst journey he had ever been on. Frank, Jay, William and Thomas had found the same difficulty when they found the shanty a few months before. They had thought it was unlivable.

The two pails caught on every branch and limb, making him think he should just leave them. But he needed the cookies and bread until he could hunt. He had his knife and pistol that he had stolen from the mercantile store. Even though he knew his father would have objected and would have taken them away from him.

Rose was up very early in the morning. She prepared a large breakfast with hot coffee, waiting for Henry's brothers to return with good news that Wilber Kolveck had been found.

The quiet manner in which each brother walked into Rose's kitchen told her that Wilber was still out there somewhere.

They were tired and almost to the point of being angry. They explained how they couldn't understand how he could be almost invisible.

Rose served them breakfast and said, "He'll get caught, we just can't give up. We'll send out word to all of our people on the Helgens' homestead to keep looking wherever they go."

Chapter 36

Blue Sky knocked softly on Rose's door. It was afternoon and she was sure Rose's children were taking their nap.

Rose opened the door and greeted Blue Sky and couldn't help but notice how happy she looked. Blue Sky was truly in love and it showed. The two friends talked in private about the secret they had shared for two years. They whispered, afraid to even talk about it. The fear they both had was the picture that Mrs. Morrison was about to receive. Would it show how Hank was changing he did not look like Mary. Rose had seen Jessie Rocker and she stated to Blue Sky, "Hank does not resemble Jessie Rocker. Jessie was light skinned."

Rose stepped close to Blue Sky to hear her say, "Rose, we must find out, who Hanks real father is. I'm thinking the family Ruby Morrison was working for had a Spanish American as a hired hand."

"But, Blue Sky, he does not look like his real mother. So we must just wait and see what Mrs. Morrison will say and do after she receives the picture."

Blue Sky walked to the door and turned to study Rose's face. She stood deep in thought.

"Rose," Blue Sky said. "When are you going to tell me?"

"Soon, I'll come to see you soon." Rose answered her.

Henry entered the cabin soon after Blue Sky left. He put his arms around Rose and held her in his strong arms and kissed her.

"I love you so much, Rose. I am so thankful you found my father's barn to get out of the rain storm." Henry sounded so sincere when he said it.

Rose raised her hands and put each hand on each of his cheeks and kissed him passionately. "I have something to tell you, Henry."

Henry pulled her thin body even closer, embracing her and kissing her long and hard. What Rose was about to tell him was what he wanted to hear. At that moment he felt he loved her more than he had ever loved her before. It was a time for them both of feeling safe and secure and completely happy. His love was forever and Rose knew it.

"The baby will be born next spring when new life begins. When the trees bud out and the flowers bloom and our baby calves will be born." Rose said with love in her heart and happiness in her voice.

"There is just one thing." Henry said.

"We will catch him" Rose said sounding sure.

Chapter 37

The kitchen and dining area work was completed after the noon meal and Walter mentioned an adventure to Wyatt, Gerrit and Brandon that he thought would be great fun for them to go on.

"I left a knife at our old home and I want to go back and get it. Do you guys want to go with me?" Walter sounded as if he was begging them to go with him.

"Sure, I do" replied Wyatt.

"I want to go" Gerrit sounded excited about going back to their old shack.

"What about helping get supper for the cowhands?" Brandon asked wanting to go but remembering how Cook handed out punishment if you didn't get your job done.

Walter was ready for any questions.

He said quickly, "I'll ask Katy, Gilda, and Abigail to help Cook."

"Okay, but we better not get into trouble." Brandon spoke meaning all of them.

"Fill your canteen and get some cookies when Cook leaves the kitchen. Get enough for all of us. We'll start now so we can be back by dark. Wear your boots, put on long sleeve shirts. Don't take anything but your canteen full of water and cookies." Walter said, in charge as usual.

Going back to the shanty meant a lot to the boys, after all they were all born there and that's the only home they had ever known until now.

Walter decided to tell one person and he was sure she would not tell.

All of the boys were laughing and slapping at each other. They snuck out behind the bunkhouse and started north.

Walter was first of course, leading the way he stood taller than Brandon. Wyatt and Gerrit were the same height. The boys were always together and they always walked in line according to age.

They entered the thick matted trees giggling this was all so familiar to them.

Walter yelled back at the boys saying, "Do you remember the fun we had with Frank"? Each one hollered "yes" remembering how they had picked on him.

They had no problem climbing over the brush, weeds and fallen tree branches and limbs.

It took the boys only two hours to get through and then they could see light coming through the open area where their old home was standing.

They all stood just staring at the shanty. Walter sat down on the ground first and then each one followed. The four boys sat in a line. They had had so much fun coming through the trees. They each loved climbing up the big trees that had many sturdy strong limbs. This had been their way of life before their family left the shanty. Each boy had jumped up and swung on the lower limbs. Coming here had felt like before, free from any responsibility.

"Let's not go back, let's just stay here forever." Gerrit said to his brothers with a big smile on his face.

"Yeah, we can swim and we can fish and hunt for our own food," Wyatt added agreeing with Gerrit.

"But what about Mother, she would miss us. Father would come and take us back to the Rose Donlin Helgens' homestead." Brandon said.

"Okay, you guys, we have to go back." Walter said knowing he would never leave his colt.

Walter stood up and took one step and the boys were upon their feet. They all followed Walter as he headed for the shanty. The roof over the door had fallen down and Walter stepped over it and the boys followed.

Each one entered the first room. No one spoke they all stood remembering their life there.

Then they all walked into the next room and nothing had changed. The boards were still covering the windows. The room was dark, but a small amount of light was coming from the open door. They all stepped into the first bedroom where their Mother and Father had slept in. The old mattress was still in the same place on the floor.

The second bedroom was down a narrow hall. No one spoke, they all just looked. Walter stepped in first and then immediately, quickly, put one arm up in the air. He turned and put his arm out on Wyatt's chest for all to step back.

Walter walked back out the way they had entered and all the boys followed him.

"Someone's sleeping in there." Walter whispered.

The boys all stared at him.

"Who is it, what are we going to do? What's he doing here? How did he get here?" Wyatt choked whispering.

Walter answered by saying, "Do you remember the guy everyone at the Rose Donlin homestead was looking for?"

"Well, I think we just found him."

"Walter, what are we going to do?" Wyatt whispered.

"Let's go back to the bunkhouse and tell Frank." Gerrit said before Walter could say, "If we took time to go back, he could be gone when we got back here."

"Did they say if he's found bring him back dead or alive?" Brandon asked in his nine year old voice.

"We need a plan, everybody think of a plan." Walter said needing help. Everyone was so excited and trying hard to help.

Gerrit said, "Let's just lock him up in the bedroom he's in." Walter turned and looked at him and said, "Gerrit, the bedroom does not have a door on it."

"If we had some rope we could tie him to a tree like we did Frank, remember?" Wyatt said.

"I'll go look for some." Brandon said in a whisper.

"No," Walter said, "We all stay together, what if he wakes up and has a gun. We will all go look for some rope."

Walter went first, the boys followed. They all hurried toward the big tree that Frank had sat down by to rest before taking the whole family back to the Rose Donlin Helgens' homestead.

Walter kicked the leaves with his foot and then leaned down and picked up the end of the rope that had been left there. They all grinned and slapped at each other.

Standing together in a circle whispering to each other on how they would tie this person up.

Walter heard all of the idea's, after all he was the oldest, being fourteen. Wyatt was thirteen and Gerrit was twelve and Brandon was the youngest boy being nine years old. Katy was in line after Gerrit then Brandon.

The boys each told Walter their idea about how to tie the stranger up that had invaded their old home.

Walter finally decided on the one he felt was best.

The afternoon had gone so fast and it would be dark soon, they couldn't go back now. They would have to stay until morning.

Chapter 38

The one person back at the bunkhouse that knew where the boys were had helped get the cowhands supper and now was getting concerned because the boys had not returned. And Walter had promised her they would be back long before darkness.

Katy loved each of her brothers, so her decision was to tell.

Frank had just started his supper when Katy asked to tell him something. He stood up and left his food on his plate, motioned for Jay, William and Thomas to saddle up.

Frank explained to his brothers what they would do, "We'll ride to the edge of the tall trees and instead of going through we'll ride fast and hard around the area like William had done when they found Harry and Berta's family. We'll come out at the creek and then walk to the shanty from there."

Chapter 39

Walter reminded the boys to be as quiet as they could because the man could get away from them if they woke him up.

Wyatt would carry the rope. Each boy knew exactly what they were to do. When they all got to the bedroom they were to run straight at the person sleeping. At the same time Walter pulled off the quilt then sat down on the sleeping man's legs.

Gerrit jumped on and straddled the man's stomach, holding down his arms to his waist. Brandon sat down on his head.

Wyatt working around all of his brothers wrapped the rope as fast as he could, starting at his feet around and around each brother moved just enough when the rope was close to them.

The man woke furious, moving and hollering but the boys held on until Wyatt had tied him all up. He worked the rope under him and the boys rolled him back and forth until the intruder couldn't move and Brandon was still sitting on his head.

The boys were completely out of breath. They all stood up and backed away and looked at the helpless man yelling at them. Each one tried hard not to show how very scared they really were.

Gerrit looked into the man's pail setting beside the man and saw the pistol and knife. They each took turns looking into the pail and realized this could have turned out badly. One of them could have been shot or stabbed.

Walter quickly took the pail outside and hid it away from the shanty in the thick bushes.

The man moaned and groaned and tried to move while yelling, "You're not playing the game right." Of course the boys had no idea what the man was talking about.

The room was getting dark and the boys all sat down around the man with their backs up against the wall. Walter motioned for Brandon to sit by him. Just to keep him safe. The boys tried to stay awake but it had been a long day and each one fell asleep.

It was just before morning and Walter woke suddenly thinking he heard someone say his name. Then he heard it again and looked out of the bedroom door and heard noises and a light was coming into the shanty.

Walter yelled, "In here." It was Frank.

Henry's four bothers walked in. Jay was holding a lantern up to see if everyone was there.

The sight of a man lying on the floor all tied up was a shock and surprise to Frank, Jay, William and Thomas. They all took turns peering down at him.

"This is not the way you play the game" the man said again, only louder to everyone in the room.

Brandon was still whispering and said, "It's him, it's him, it's the man Henry and Rose are looking for."

With a smile on his face, Frank, said "I think your right Brandon, but we have never seen him only heard about him."

Frank continued saying, "Okay boys we're riding double and I'll take the man on my horse and his gun and knife."

Before they all got on their horse each boy shared their cookies they had left at the tree edge and also they emptied out the man's cookies from his pail. They drank from their canteen then climbed on the horses for the trip back to the homestead. Two of the smallest brothers rode with Thomas one boy on the saddle with Thomas and one behind the saddle. The young boys dosed most of the way.

Frank was in front and he rode slowly. It took most of the morning before they were in sight of the homestead.

As the group of horses rode up toward the cabin, Henry came out onto the wrap-around porch and stood looking. He could see them off in the distance. Rose followed carrying Joseph with Paul, Margaret and Myra right behind. They all watched the horses and riders come closer.

Henry stood like a statue staring, he couldn't take his eyes off of the first rider and the man sitting in front all tied up.

Henry stood stiff and he leaned forward with his hands turning white clutching the porch railing. He was a large strong man but the memories were flooding back.

He was remembering falling into the swollen fast moving currant and being dragged under. Wilber Kolveck had saved his life, and then committed a crime by kidnapping him.

Rose stepped over and put her arm around Henry's waist. She felt his body tremble. She had never seen Wilber but Henry's reaction told her who this man was.

Rose spoke first and said, "We need to send for Sheriff Les now."

Everyone dismounted including Frank. He left Wilber sitting in the saddle with his hands tied to the saddle horn. They would never give Wilber a chance to escape.

"Is it him?" Frank said directly to Henry.

After Frank asked the question, no one made a sound. It seemed as if the horses stood very still. Everyone was waiting for Henry's answer.

"It's him." Henry answered with his teeth together and his fists clinched. "Send for Sheriff Les."

Everyone turned and looked at Wilber with sober faces when he shouted loudly, "This is not how you play the game."

Jay offered to go for the Sheriff. His love of riding fast would get the Sheriff to Henry and Rose's cabin within the hour.

Frank needed to get Wilber away from Henry. "I'll tell you everything later" he said referring to how Wilber was found. He walked his horse with Wilber still tied to the saddle horn down to the corral to wait for Sheriff Les.

Rose took Henry and the children into the cabin immediately. Inga was instructed by Rose to keep the children in the cabin and read to them while she was gone. Inga was also instructed Henry was not to leave the cabin even if she had to sit on him. She agreed she could do that.

All of the brothers were ready to take their horses to the corral and remove the saddles. Eating was all the young boys could think of. Cook motioned for the boys to get a plate while he put food on each one.

Chapter 40

Rose needed to tell Dora Kolveck before the Sheriff sent one of his deputies to tell her. She sent for her horse, hoping to make it a fast trip. It would not be long and it would be night time. Rose was not afraid to travel home in the dark. Her magnificent horse had traveled many miles with her traveling across Missouri when Henry brought her to Oklahoma City from his family's farm.

Rose tried to think of ways to tell Dora and also tell her she would help get Wilber on some medicine. Dora would never be free from him. She would always be responsible for him and need to care for him.

The night air was cool and she was glad her cape was wool and very warm covering her entire body. The hood covered her hair and was around most of her face. The sounds she could hear were all sounds of the night time, from large and small birds. Coyotes were howling. Little animals ran fast across the trail to keep from being stepped on by the huge feet of her horse.

She and Henry had waited a long time to be completely free of Wilber. There had been a big black cloud over them and now it had been lifted.

The big white house came into view. Rose tied her giant horse to the railing in front of the house.

She was just about to knock when Dora opened the door. Dora's greeting was warm and she invited Rose in for coffee.

The two women sat across from each other. One waiting to hear what the other came to tell her and hoping she could tell Dora without her becoming hysterical about her brother being in jail.

Rose said, "Dora, I have very good news for you. Wilber has been found unharmed. He will be in the custody of Sheriff Les at the jail."

Dora jumped to her feet and yelled, almost a scream, "I need to see Wilber now, I must go." Her eyes were large and her face turned red.

"No no, Dora, you need to wait until morning Wilber needs to rest tonight, and I'll go with you." Rose wondered why she had said that, but Dora was all alone. She had no one but Wilber.

"I'll meet you there in the morning" Rose repeated again.

Slowly Dora sat down relieved to hear Wilber was not hurt.

"Drink your coffee Rose, "I'm going to get some fruit for us. My bread and cookies are all gone again."

Rose sat and waited for Dora to return. The minutes slipped by and finally Dora came into the kitchen with a jar of fruit and several empty jars.

Dora stood looking puzzled over the empty jars. She had not been to the basement for fruit for a long time.

Rose asked, "Has someone else been in your fruit room?"

"No no, I don't think so. I have never heard anyone down there." Dora answered slowly.

"Maybe I should look for you." Rose stood up and walked to the basement door. Dora lit her lantern again and walked first down the steps. Dora took Rose into the fruit room and discovered more empty jars.

Rose was standing behind Dora, while they both searched the shelves. Rose looked down at the trunk setting next to the wall. She was admiring the old decorations and carvings on it. Then she noticed a very small space behind it. Also there were small bits of dirt on the floor by the edge of the trunk. Rose leaned over and looked closer at the space behind the trunk and the wall. With both hands on the trunk she pulled it away from the wall.

"Here," Rose said to Dora, motioning for her to hold the lantern closer. It was the tunnel.

Rose pushed the trunk away so the hole was completely open for them both to look into. Dora did not act surprised as she said, "It's an old tunnel Wilber and I found after our parents died."

"But where does it go?" Rose asked curiously.

"I don't know because I refused to enter it. But Wilber crawled into it." Dora said innocently.

"Dora, has Wilber been using this tunnel to hide in?" Before Dora could answer Rose said, "Hold the lantern closer, I see something. I can see a shovel, some clothes, a razor."

Dora's voice sounded afraid. "He's been hiding in here for a long time and I did not know it. That's where my bread and cookies disappeared to."

"Oh Rose, I must close up this tunnel so he can never use it again." Dora said it in a whisper.

"We must find the other end and close that up too." Rose answered her in a whisper.

"But how, who is going to crawl through the tunnel?" Dora asked sounding tired and worried. Then continued, saying "I just can't."

"I'll do it" Rose said in barely a whisper.

"What, what did you say?" Dora turned completely around and looked at Rose.

Rose spoke again, trying to make her words sound confident. "I'll go through the tunnel."

"No, Rose." Before Dora could finish Rose said. "Dora, take the lantern into the barn and stand with it where you guess the tunnel would come out."

"Keep shouting my name Dora." Rose instructed.

Rose held her dress up and proceeded to remove her slip. She tucked her skirt hem into her bloomers. The slip she wrapped around her neck in case she needed to cover her mouth and also keep dirt from sliding down in the inside of her dress.

Rose needed to do this in a hurry before she changed her mind. A couple steps and she was at the dark tunnel. Bending down on her hands and knees, stared into the darkness.

The tunnel felt cool at first but Rose was trying to crawl fast. Once deep inside the tunnel a few feet she began to feel different.

Suddenly the smell of stale musty dirt made her feel nauseated and breathing was becoming difficult. The faster she moved the more dust was in the air. Rose stopped and lifted her slip over her mouth. For a moment she was not sure she would get through the tunnel. She tried pretending Henry and the children were waiting for her at the end of the tunnel.

Little pieces of loose dirt fell from the top of the tunnel. Rose tried to keep the thought of the tunnel collapsing on her out of her mind.

Rose guessed she was half way through when her knees began to burn, she pictured them bleeding. Her hands felt hard pebbles cutting and digging in.

She stopped to catch her breath. The tunnel was completely black and no matter how many times she blinked, black was all she could see.

Rose started slower this time and continued on. It seemed it felt as if the tunnel had been in a straight line. But now it felt the tunnel was leading into a curve and it made her feel she had made a wrong turn. She began to feel anxious and her heart was racing.

Dora had been calling again and again without Rose hearing her.

Suddenly Rose heard her name being called. She called back in a loud whisper, "I'm coming, I'm coming," fearing the tunnel would cave in on her.

Dora heard Rose's voice and it sounded as if it was coming from the manger. She held the lantern in the manger and at the end, next to the barn wall were boards pounded together looking like a gate. Dora had never noticed it before.

Lifting up the boards, they came straight up, and behind the gate was the tunnel.

Dora half cried while saying, "Rose."

Rose crawled out into the manger. After the gate was closed, the two women embraced.

Chapter 41

Rose slipped into her woolen cape and mounted her horse for a fast ride home.

Rose could not forget Dora's loving embrace. She wanted to make life better for Dora but Wilber would always come first.

As Rose rode closer to her cabin she saw a small light glowing on her porch. She knew Henry was waiting up for her.

Henry reached up and lifted Rose off of her horse and pulled her into his waiting arms. She wrapped her arms around his neck feeling safe and secure. Nothing like the feeling she had had in the tunnel.

Henry took her giant horse to the stable while Rose washed up. Removing the dust and dirt to stopped the anguish of the memory of the terrible stifling ordeal of crawling through the secret passage.

Rose lay in Henry's arms trying to explain why she felt Dora needed help when Wilber was released from jail.

Rose said, "I won't be there long. I need to help Dora give Wilber his medicine."

Henry's answer was trying to convince Rose how dangerous Wilber could be. He said, "Rose, I love you so much and thinking of something happening to you I just couldn't stand it."

Rose was beginning to doubt her decision to go. She closed her eyes feeling love and contentment with her life with Henry and her beautiful children. Maybe the risk would not be worth being in danger.

The morning came extremely early for Rose after crawling through the tunnel. She always started her day taking time with each of her children, lifting them into her arms while they smiled and stretch. She loved hugging and kissing them.

Breakfast was a time for Henry and Rose to show their family how much each one was loved. It was a time to listen to Paul and Margaret wanting to talk at the same time. Myra was saying words, sometimes having to repeat each word several times before being clear.

Joseph wanted to be heard just like his brother and sisters. He made sounds trying to say words in between gurgling with swinging hands and arms in the air.

The talking and giggling blocked out Sheriff Les' knocking. He opened the door and was in the kitchen before Henry and Rose was aware of him.

"I've delivered Wilber to Dora. I helped her clean him up, shaved him and cut his hair. We gave him the medicine the Dr. at the Kolveck settlement wanted him to have." He went on to say.

"Wilber was in his room going to sleep when I left. I told Dora I would be back after I came to see you. Dora is a very nice lady. She is kind and gentle and Wilber is a burden on her."

Sheriff Les looked at Henry, then said "Dora is so sorry she was part of Wilber's abduction and his unkind treatment of you."

"I'm sending my deputies to fill in the tunnel. Dora informed me about it. Wilber will never get the chance to use it ever again." Sheriff Les said it with assurance and confidence.

Henry and Rose glanced at each other realizing and hoping the problem of Wilber would be taken care of by Dora and Sheriff Les.

Chapter 42

Blue Sky made a surprise visit to the photographer's office knowing he could refuse to let her see Hank's pictures before he sent them to the Morrison family.

The photographer refused at first until Blue Sky told him she was a good friend of Toby and Mary.

The pictures were laid out in a long line in front of her. Blue Sky studied each one very carefully. Each picture showed a different look of Hank. This was a welcomed sight. Blue Sky thought Hank was darker than the other children Mary had had. But who could prove anything.

Blue Sky needed to tell Rose the pictures would not reveal anything to the Morrison family to use to try and get Hank away from Mary and Toby.

The other situation was to check Rose because of her babies was coming so close together in time.

Chapter 43

Cook had started praising any of the squatter children when they helped in any way to help him prepare the meals each day.

But when he started paying the ones with a penny that helped, he had no idea how determined and persistent to have something they had never had before.

After each child learned about the pennies being given for working, at 4:00 a.m. the following morning all of the ten children of Harry and Berta showed up to help get the breakfast ready.

The older children helped the younger siblings, so everyone would get something they had never had in their hand, a penny.

Each child would not take more pennies than his or her siblings. They wanted each to have the same amount.

The older boys, Walter, Gerrit, Wyatt and Brandon carried the plates and silverware out for the cowhands to pick-up and fill their plates with potatoes and scrambled eggs while Katy, Stella and Abigail buttered toast.

Gilda, Martha and Betsy laid the toast on the cowhand's plates. Cook heard no complaints, and Harry and Berta were smiling all through breakfast.

Frank, Jay, William and Thomas all walked in together. Frank came in being friendly to everyone. He spoke to all of the young boys calling them by name, even though they had pulled so many tricks on him. But the boys caught Wilber so they were okay. They had all the rights to the story when it was told.

William started moving the kitchen pans around as usual, and then started teasing Thomas about Katy.

Jay filled his plate and sat down and ate everything on his plate, he just sat and watched thinking this is all family.

Breakfast was over, the kitchen cleaned and Cook brought out a small bag. He laid out the pennies for the older children, for the three youngest, he laid in each small hand a penny. The girls Abigail, Martha and Betsy looked down at their pennies as if they were gold.

...story to be continued...